Life Rescued

By

Sandy Graham

Books by Sandy Graham

Pillage Trilogy
  Life Shattered
  Life Rescued
  Life Threatened

Murder – On Saltspring?
The Pizza Dough King
Speak For Me
A Quiet Rampage

Published in the United States of America

ISBN: 9798456821560

Dedication

"Life Rescued" is dedicated to Sheila (Sharpe) Graham, the "big sister" in spirit rather than birth. In her subtle way she steered me through perilous potholes in my early twenties. And over the years helped plant the seed that led me to plunge into creative writing by offering encouragement and gentle suggestions.

Early versions of "Life Shattered" had Delbert dying in front of Sylvia with her pining to death six months later. Buried side by side, they were united in death but not in life. Sheila found a way to make me see it was too brutal an ending and praised the current version, saying she now cried happily through the final two chapters. Without her guidance, the story of Delbert and Sylvia would have been dead-ended and this sequel impossible.

Sheila, though we are poorer for your departure, you live on in spirit and remain a positive influence on many lives.

Author's Note

This story was originally published under the title "Two Loves Sought" which apparently led some to expect a romance novel. It is a literary novel which crosses the genres of romance, young adult and historical fiction.

Chapter 1

When Delbert Pillage crash landed his jet fighter on Royal Colwood Golf Course, he saved lives, but it cost him both feet and left him paralyzed from the waist down. In those first days, he fought for life because the accident brought back Sylvia Cairns. But to what? A broken man with half a body?

As days went by, her love and constant nursing became a beacon for him. She quelled the self-doubts generated by sharp pains in his back and sometimes others that seemed to shoot from his imaginary feet. But would he ever have a life again? A worthwhile life?

In a way it reminded him of his youth, tormented by bullies, defended by Sylvia. Back then, he learned to cope with the harassment and grow into his potential through Sylvia's gentle support and encouragement. Even when he lost her, he strove to be worthy of her faith in him. And through his intelligence, succeeded beyond their expectations. Now the injury and pain tortured him and dashed his chances of flying again. Though the crash reunited them, how could he give her the life she deserved? That question became intense when she wanted to get married.

"I can't burden you with taking care of me, always limited in what you can do."

Her impassioned response shocked him.

"Over the past three years I have longed to be with you. It never went away. I came to realize I made three bad mistakes;

failing to avoid the rape, botching the abortion and, most important in hindsight, not letting you decide your own course of action. It's wrong to make other people's decisions for them. When a man proposes to a woman he has already made up his mind. All that remains for her is to accept or reject the proposal. I'm proposing to you, Delbert, will you marry me?"

He had followed his heart and mumbled yes. From that moment on, he determined to ignore the signs of pity that fluttered across people's faces and refused to consider himself disabled. For her sake he would make the most of his new situation.

Now married, they delighted in each other's company. The trials through which each persevered heightened their joy each day together, almost a honeymoon without end. It did have a beginning, however. Publicly marked by their August 1960 wedding on Salt Spring Island, which captivated local residents and left them with talking fodder for years to come. Privately, it was not so clearly delineated. In the weeks leading up to the wedding, Delbert recovered from a back operation which left his fourth and fifth lumbar vertebrae held together by a metal rod over his severely damaged spinal cord. He was very much a patient and Sylvia his nurse. They kissed and gently hugged but that was the extent of their intimacy.

By the wedding day, Delbert was out of a back brace and free to do whatever he could. They discovered a more intimate relationship both possible and thrilling. Yet, though his happiness was genuine when together, Delbert often succumbed to depression when alone. He felt robbed of so much of his previous lifestyle.

Sylvia caught him in one of those moods as he sat staring out the window at a persistent drizzle. She quietly walked up behind, put her arms around him and whispered in his ear.

"A penny for your thoughts."

He leaned his cheek against hers. "That would be a poor investment."

"Let me decide."

"You want to hear confession, Sister Sylvia?"

She jabbed him good-naturedly in the ribs. "Yes, if that's what you want to call it."

He paused. "You give me such joy it's not right to express sadness but try as I might, I can't always ignore what the accident took away."

"Like flying?"

"Flying and more. Life with the Martin's opened my eyes. Dan taught me to fly. Charlie taught me the value of exercise. I became convinced that both physical and mental activity are crucial for one's well-being. Now both are lost."

"Compromised, not lost."

"Seriously compromised."

"That's up to you."

"I have a forlorn hope that somehow my spinal cord will heal itself and I will walk again with artificial feet. Maybe even run."

Sylvia felt strangled by a wave of sadness. She fought to conceal it. He needed direction, not commiseration.

"Didn't the doctors say the damage was permanent?"

"Yes."

"Then we should find new physical and mental activities for you. Let any feeling regained be an unexpected miracle."

"I'll try."

As the days passed, Sylvia helped Delbert when needed yet subtly encouraged him to do as much as possible for himself. That proved easy since he was driven to avoid placing a burden on anyone, least of all her. His priority became development of upper body strength in order to gain mobility in and out of his wheelchair. A reasonable goal fraught with unanticipated challenges which frequently left him dejected by the lack of progress.

Just learning how to climb into the chair proved difficult. To dress himself he had to bend far forward to pull underwear and pants over even his shortened legs. Then lean from side to side to work them up. Bathroom visits were harder to master. He had a bar installed to help swing himself between chair and toilet. The room design did not cater to his needs. Still, with perseverance he developed a successful technique.

In his previous life with feet, he enjoyed a ten kilometer run most days. He missed that almost as much as his feet. At Sylvia's suggestion, he laid out a route for a daily morning roll on the sidewalks of Victoria. From their apartment on Rockland Avenue, it headed north to Oak Bay Avenue, east to Newport and south to Beach Drive. The stretch along Beach Drive would give a spectacular view of the coastline before it split off onto Fairfield Road. Then the route headed north on St Charles to Fort Street and back onto Oak Bay Avenue for the return to their apartment. Just over seven kilometers with a hilly part in the last half.

"That a long circuit," Sylvia cautioned when he described it to her. "Shouldn't you start with something shorter?"

"I have to challenge myself to get the full benefit."

Resigned, Sylvia watched him set off. The first third was a gentle down slope. Easy going and Delbert made good time though it did little for his muscles. The second third along the coast required significantly more exertion in return for the view.

When he turned up St Charles the situation changed abruptly. The effort required to roll uphill far exceeded his expectation. He ground to a halt in half a block, exhausted, turned sideways and set the brake. The hill now looked like a mountain.

His breathing returned to normal after five minutes, so he turned and started up. Within a hundred feet, he gasped for air again. His arms and shoulders ached. *What was I thinking? I'm not going to make it.* It took a longer rest this time.

The third stretch showed mercy on him with a shallower grade. He made a full block before the next rest stop. Then it steepened once more. At the next pause to gather what strength he had left, it looked impossible.

I should have run in the other direction. It would be a long shallow climb that way. Maybe I should turn back even now. Do I have enough energy to make it all the way around?

Sylvia must have started to worry. She'll come this way to find me. If I go back, she'll chase me all the way around. Have to press on. He began to push on the wheels. Arms rubbery and aching from the exertion, he made it less than a hundred feet before the next stop.

When she came over the crest of the hill, Sylvia spotted him hunched over, head bowed. She called to him.

"Delbert! What happened? Are you alright?"

He gave her a small wave and waited, humiliated. He cried on the inside but struggled not to show it.

"This hill is too much for me. I should have gone in the other direction."

"You overdo it, dear."

"I feel so helpless. Doomed to never climb slopes. Such a burden on you."

"You're a joy, not a burden. It takes time to build your strength."

"Maybe more than a lifetime."

"You don't need to become a Charles Atlas overnight. Nobody kicks sand in your face."

"I'm sorry. I wish I had your patience."

"Let's see if two person-power can conquer the hill."

With Sylvia pushing and Delbert working the wheels they made steady progress. At the top, they both panted to regain breath. Then set off at a leisurely pace for home.

Recovered now, Delbert thanked her for the rescue.

"You're right, I need to recognize it takes time and focus on a gradual build-up."

"The day will come when you can muscle your way up hills like that."

"In the meantime, I'll run in the other direction."

"You mean roll. But I wish you would start with an easier route."

"I can handle this one in that direction and it'll make me stronger quicker."

Sylvia sighed. There was no way to hold him back.

Chapter 2

Within two weeks he rolled the route without rest stops. The challenge became the time it took. Then one morning he announced he would try it in the harder direction.

"Why?"

"To prove I can do it now. If I'm not back in an hour come find me on the hill."

It took two rest stops, but he made it around. One of the endless challenges he would face was conquered. Of those that remained, he was particularly concerned with the atrophy of his legs. He knew the danger of blood clots, skin sores and brittle bones from lack of circulation. Sylvia was taken aback when he said he needed a way to exercise his legs.

"What on earth are you talking about?"

"I'm serious. I need a way to move my legs with my arms. Movement is necessary to circulate blood and keep at least a little muscle activity."

"Honey, you're not a contortionist. Do you want me to move them back and forth or massage them?"

"No. I'm already a chain around your neck. I want to unburden you, not enslave you. I have an idea for an exercise machine using bicycle parts."

It sounded weird but Sylvia welcomed a project for him to tackle. What emerged looked like a bicycle chain drive with pedals at each end.

"See, we would attach these pedals to my stumps. When I crank this end, my legs will move back and forth as if they pedaled a bicycle. If nothing else, it will give me arm and shoulder exercise. I think it will decrease the atrophy in my legs and improve circulation down there as well."

"Guess if it doesn't cause pain, it might help."

"The pains I feel will occur just like they do now. It won't affect them."

"Who would build this contraption?"

"A bicycle repair shop should be able to build the first Pillage Exercise Contraption."

He laughed which made her follow suit. Together they measured the dimensions needed to fit him sitting in his wheelchair. A search through the yellow pages revealed an outfit that prided itself on custom built bikes. After lunch they paid a visit.

The man behind the counter had a neatly trimmed beard and leathery face from a life in wind and sun. Of medium height, thin and wiry, it was easy to imagine him cycling a hundred miles a day, up hills and down. He sprang from behind the counter with infectious enthusiasm.

"Hi folks, I'm Tony. How can I help you? A bike for you, Ma'am?"

Delbert responded, "Not at this time. Can you build this?"

"What is it?"

"An exercise machine which will let me work my paralyzed legs."

Tony studied the sketch.

"You want it to move your legs when you pedal it with your hands?"

"You got it."

"We need to gear it so it doesn't move them too fast when you pedal comfortably." He laughed. "Guess we should call them carpels instead of pedals."

Delbert laughed. Sylvia didn't.

"Sure, I think I can piece this together. You happy with the dimensions?"

"Yes."

"One thing I'm not clear about is how the lower pedals will attach to your legs. Would it be okay for me to take a look at them?"

Delbert pulled his pants up to show his stubs. Tony nodded and thanked him.

"It will cost between three and four hundred bucks."

"That's fine."

"Give me your phone number and a week, maybe two if I get busy."

* * *

It took a week and a day to hear back. Delbert had become anxious, afraid he was not taken seriously. Tony sounded excited over the phone though he probably always did, given his boundless energy.

"Your machine is ready for a trial run."

"Great. We'll be over in an hour."

Delbert recognized it sitting in the corner as soon as they entered. He wheeled to it, impressed with Tony's professional workmanship. In no way did it look kludged. Tony had set it on a wider base than expected. That allowed Delbert to easily wheel into position. Tony lifted his legs and inserted them into cup shaped receptacles mounted on the lower pedals.

Delbert grasped the upper pedals or carpels as Tony called them. When he began to crank, one leg was pushed up but the other simply slid out of its cup.

"Damn," Tony exclaimed, "I forgot you can't push back. We need to fasten your legs to the pedals. Hold on, I'll make straps."

He was a few minutes in back before returning with two short buckled straps.

"This is not a solution but it will let us test the gear ratio. What I need to do is replace the cups with a longer, padded support to rest your leg on. Then use two straps to hold it. This might hurt."

Delbert laughed. "That's one thing it won't do. I like your idea for attaching them."

With the legs more or less fastened to the cups, Delbert was able to work the exerciser. Pedaling felt comfortable and leg motion was at a safe speed. Both men were pleased. Sylvia watched, still skeptical about the whole thing.

"Come back tomorrow about this time and I'll have it finished. By the way, it comes apart so you can break it down for transport home."

* * *

When they got it home, Delbert started right in pedalling. Sylvia heard it whirring away from the kitchen. After almost an hour she interceded.

"Don't overdo it. Work up gradually."

"Okay, I'll call it a day. Feels good. Actually more beneficial than the circuit."

A week of using the device daily convinced Sylvia of its value too. His legs had more color, circulation improved. A plus in his mind was the additional exercise it provided for his upper body.

He kept secret the other ache in his heart—flying. At times he dreamed he was back in the cockpit of the Avro Arrow. He could feel the tremendous thrust pushing him back in his seat, see the control panel with the altimeter spinning up at an unprecedented rate. Then the pain signals sent from his damaged body would wake him. It left him to fight the ensuing depression. *Why am I afflicted with pain from the part of my body that has no feeling?* He knew they were secondary signals but that didn't help. *Am I doomed to spend the rest of my life like this?*

At these times he needed Sylvia's calming influence, but he burdened her too much already. Just the thought of her love and devotion carried him through the darkest hours. *In many ways I'm a lucky man. If only I could still fly an airplane.*

Chapter 3

On Friday morning he wheeled along Fort Street, focused on the sidewalk ahead. Out of the corner of his eye he spotted a person huddled in the shadows between two buildings. It was just a glimpse, but it left him with an impression of someone in trouble. He braked to a stop, spun around and headed back to investigate.

A young girl sat, her back against the building. She appeared to be in the fifteen to seventeen range. Provocatively dressed but grubby. Her long blonde hair showed signs of neglect. She cried silently and shook uncontrollably.

"May I help you?"

Her eyes attempted to focus on the wheelchair and its occupant.

"Can you help yourself?"

Delbert ignored her sass. "Are you lost?"

"Yes, more than you'll ever know. Just leave me alone."

"You're in drug withdrawal, aren't you?"

"Why don't you mind your own business…if you want to help, give me twenty dollars. I'd offer sex in return but I can see that wouldn't interest you."

He ignored the dig. "To buy more drugs?"

"Oh, fuck off mister. You're no help."

"When did you last eat?"

"Leave me alone!"

"I won't contribute to your habit, but my wife and I can feed you and help you get treatment."

"Now a fucking cripple wants to help me. Why don't you worry about helping yourself?"

"I do. Every day."

"You want to throw me in a drug tank. No way."

"I was thinking of something more productive, like methadone treatment."

"When that's over I'll be right back here again."

"Perhaps, but a meal and bath right now is better than lying in the gutter, shaking and crying. Come on."

He turned and started to wheel away, then stopped after fifty feet. She stared at him, gave him the finger. He beckoned her to follow and waited. After a few minutes that seemed much longer, she slowly stood up and walked toward him. He moved on again at a walking pace. She tagged along behind.

* * *

Sylvia became concerned. He was taking longer than usual to complete the loop. *Has he fallen or been hit by a car?* She started to trace his route backwards. As she turned the corner onto Fort Street, he came into view. He moved slowly toward her. Something was wrong. *Has he wrenched a shoulder? I wish he wasn't so aggressive with that chair.*

For the first time, she noticed the waif who walked half a dozen paces behind, as if led on a rope. *Is there a connection?*

Does she plan to attack him? He waved when he saw her. *Does he know the girl follows him?* She hurried to meet them.

"Hi dear. We have company for breakfast."

He turned to the girl. "This is my wife, Sylvia. My name is Delbert. What's yours?"

"Cynthia."

She stared at Sylvia, nervous, still trembling yet in awe of the woman's beauty. Sylvia's warm smile seemed to comfort her.

"Hello Cynthia. Come on. Our place is just a couple of blocks over on Rockland Avenue."

Sylvia moved behind the wheelchair to push, then thought better of it.

"Lead on Master," she said with a laugh.

He did, Sylvia and Cynthia in tow.

"Is that as fast as you can go?"

He sped up and soon the two females were trotting in a vain effort to keep pace. They both laughed when they reached the apartment, breathless. For a moment the tremors were gone but not for long. Sylvia put her arm around the girl in a semi hug and led her inside. The shaking became more violent.

"This won't work. I need a fix. Let me go and leave you alone."

Sylvia held her tightly.

"It will pass. You need food too."

Delbert was on the phone.

"Doctor Hanson, Delbert Pillage here. I have an unusual request. Perhaps you can point me in the right direction. We came across a teenager suffering from drug withdrawal. Can you help us get her into methadone treatment?"

He listened for a while, then said, "Yes, I'll hang on."

Finally, "Okay, outpatient clinic at the Jubilee. Thank you."

"The cops took me there once. When I wouldn't tell them about my parents, they just sent me to Child Welfare. You may mean well but you're wasting your time."

"We'll say we're your guardians and take responsibility for you."

"Why?"

"Because we can't stand by while a young girl throws her life away," Sylvia interjected, "like I almost did."

That caught Cynthia's attention. *How could this beautiful woman have ever been in a situation like mine?*

"We need to make you more presentable before we go to the clinic. I know you're in pain now. Can you take a bath while Sylvia cooks breakfast?"

"I need a fix so bad."

"I know dear," Sylvia said. "Come with me. I'll run the bath."

When Sylvia returned to the kitchen, she told Delbert the girl shook so badly she almost splashed water out of the tub. She handed him his razor blades for safe-keeping and started on their breakfast.

"Perhaps soaking in hot water will relax her a bit."

"She's a pretty girl. What a shame. They always target the attractive ones."

Fifteen minutes later breakfast was ready. No sign of Cynthia. Sylvia decided to check on her. She tapped lightly on the door.

"Cynthia?"

No answer. Alarmed, she called louder. Still no answer. She opened the door. Cynthia was lying with her head under water. Sylvia screamed, rushed in and pulled her head up. The girl was unconscious. She dragged her out of the tub onto the floor face down. Alternately pressing down on her shoulder blades and pulling up on her elbows first pumped out water. Finally, there was a cough, a gasp, another cough. Gradually Cynthia regained consciousness.

Delbert watched, helpless. *Could I have done that without Sylvia here? Don't know.* He rolled to the bedroom to get a blanket. Sylvia was drying the girl. She wrapped the blanket around her, then sat on the floor and hugged her while the girl cried. The tremors began again before the tears stopped.

"Why didn't you just let me go?" she whimpered.

"You're too valuable to lose."

"No. I'm worthless."

Delbert chimed in, "I know a girl who once felt that way. She now loves life every day. That can be your future too. Let's eat."

Sylvia half carried her wrapped in the blanket to the kitchen table and held a glass of orange juice for her to sip. The tremors nearly rendered it impossible. She could munch on a piece of cinnamon toast, liberally coated with sugar. After that,

Sylvia coaxed her to eat some scrambled egg and drink a little tea. Delbert watched them as he ate and occasionally offered encouragement. The food eaten wasn't much to nourish her but it would at least stave off starvation.

After breakfast, Sylvia took her to the bedroom in search of clean clothes that might fit. Most things were a size too large but eventually they found some Capri pants and a top that worked. Cynthia noticed a nun's habit hanging in the corner of the closet.

"Why's that there?" she asked pointing.

"I was once a novitiate."

"What's that?"

"A person training for the Sisterhood."

"You wanted to be a nun?"

"It's a long, sad story, Cynthia. I'll tell it to you sometime."

The shakes had subsided slightly, either because of the food or the distraction or both. The girl combed her hair. They went outside to find Delbert already perched in the back seat, his wheelchair beside the open door. Sylvia folded and stowed it in the trunk. Cynthia closed the back door and climbed into the front.

"You look great," Delbert commented.

"Not exactly my style of wardrobe but at least she didn't make me wear the habit."

She chuckled between shakes. He laughed. *Under it all, she's a clever girl. So much to offer, so much taken away. Can we restore her?* Sylvia backed out and they were on their way to the hospital. Each had doubts about the success of their venture.

Chapter 4

It dawned on Delbert he knew nothing about Cynthia other than her first name.

"Cynthia, to pose as your guardians we need to know more about you. What's your full name?"

"Cynthia Miriam Adams."

"Where's home?"

"Fort Street, sometimes Johnson Street."

"Very funny. Before that."

"Campbell River. My father and mother split. My father's a logger. My mother works in a restaurant kitchen. Neither wants to see me."

"We need a plausible connection. Do you know anyone on Salt Spring Island?"

She shuddered violently. He wondered why. Obviously it struck a nerve. She gathered herself, a tear in her eye.

"My father's younger brother lives there," she said barely above a whisper.

"What's his name?"

"Luke."

He'd heard of Luke Adams. Rough, foul-mouthed, known mainly for the brawls he continually started.

"Luke had a part in what's happened to you," he suggested gently. She nodded slightly.

"That will be our connection. You were sent to Luke after your parents broke up. He mistreated you and we found you and took over."

"For how long?" Skepticism in her voice.

"One thing you will learn about Delbert is that he will persevere through all kinds of hell once he puts his mind to it."

Cynthia was silent. She wanted to believe that but life had dealt her too many blows. This would probably turn into one more. In the meantime, the pain of withdrawal crowded everything else out. She desperately wanted to escape back downtown, find a pusher and promise anything for a fix.

Sylvia found a parking space in front of the outpatient clinic. As she brought the wheelchair around and opened the door for Delbert, Cynthia got out, looked around, then started to run down the street. Delbert heaved himself into the chair and took off after her. The girl was no match for Delbert's speed. He caught her a block away, grabbed her arm. She tried to pull away. He had too strong a grip.

"Let me go!"

"What frightened you, Cynthia?" he said in a soft voice.

"I don't want to go through with this. I just need a fix."

"And another and another until it finally kills you?"

"Yes."

"I know it's tough, but there can be a brighter future. You have to fight for it."

"Oh shit, you just won't give up, will you?"

"No, I won't. Let's go back and find out what they have to say."

Sylvia caught up to them and watched the exchange. She put an arm around the girl and turned her back toward the clinic. The tremors were violent again. Cynthia sobbed in agony. It tore at Delbert's heart. He marveled at Sylvia's firm yet compassionate demeanor.

This time they made it to the door. Sylvia held onto the girl inside while Delbert managed his way through the entrance. A nurse came forward to help them.

"This is Cynthia Adams," Delbert said. "We found her in withdrawal, as you can see. We want to discuss methadone treatment with you."

"You're not her parents?"

"No. Her parents split up and sent her to her uncle. He abused her and started her on drugs. We're taking over as her guardians. She will live with us."

"We need parents' consent for a minor."

"Her parents are in Campbell River. They abandoned her."

The nurse addressed the girl. "Are these people your guardians now?"

Cynthia looked at Delbert, then Sylvia. She seemed to collect her thoughts, weigh her options. Finally, still shaking she answered in a low, halting voice.

"Yes."

Delbert smiled and released the breath he held. It was a new beginning for her.

"We need to build up the methadone level gradually until we reach a dosage that fully counters the heroin urge. In fact, we will give you only five milligrams now and watch for any adverse reaction. Then you can have another five. Every other day you increase the dosage by ten milligrams until you're back to normal. Then you maintain that level. Do you want to start treatment?"

"Yes," Delbert answered before Cynthia could respond.

The nurse brought the first pill and a glass of water.

"Take this and then you must sit in the lounge for an hour."

Cynthia took the pill and Sylvia led her to a sofa.

The hour dragged on. Cynthia wanted to bolt. Sylvia hugged her and tried to sooth her. At times the shakes evolved into shudders. Sylvia held her tight. Delbert requested water from the nurse for her. She drank some. Periodically, the nurse checked her condition and stroked her brow.

"Everything looks okay with the medicine so far. We'll give you more soon, dear."

The nurse motioned Delbert to follow her back to the desk.

"This is the hardest part of my job, watching them suffer so much. I wish we could give a strong dosage right off the bat."

"Do many patients have a reaction?"

"It's a small percentage, enough that we can't take a chance."

She gave Delbert bottles of five, ten and twenty milligram pills, with a stern admonishment to keep control of them and the dosage. He must return for more before they run out.

"When that happens depends on the level she needs. She should take the pills the same time each day and never miss a day. I suggest taking them each morning after breakfast."

"Okay."

"When it looks like she can make it for twenty-four hours with only a little reaction, reduce the increase to five milligrams every other day. We want to reach a level where she has no craving, however, stop at that point. Do not go above one hundred milligrams a day no matter what. Also, do not reduce the level without consulting a doctor. Don't be disappointed if she has to take methadone for the rest of her life."

"Is there no hope of getting off it later on?"

"She may be able to transition off but it's a slow process and requires a lifestyle change which diverts her attention to positive pursuits. Her youth is in her favor in that respect."

"Reorienting her life will be our challenge."

"She's lucky to have you. So many have no one to keep them off the streets."

When the hour elapsed, Cynthia got another five milligrams. They thanked the nurse and left.

On the road, Cynthia stated, "This is a load of crap. Those pills do nothing."

"It takes time to build up the dosage to a point where your craving disappears. But it will be worth the pain you go through the next little while."

"No it won't. Let me go back to the street."

"Even now you're not shaking as much as you were."

"It hurts," she moaned.

Sylvia commiserated, "I know dear. Some lunch will help."

Both adults wondered if they could keep her against her will. Were they fighting a lost cause?

Chapter 5

Back home, Sylvia urged her to pick a soup from their selection. Scotch broth was chosen and soon warmed on the stove. Sylvia made sandwiches and cut up carrot and celery wedges. Cynthia had calmed down somewhat. Still, Delbert positioned himself discreetly between her and the door.

When lunch was served, Cynthia turned to Delbert. "You can stop guarding the door now. I'm not going to make a run for it."

Delbert laughed, "It looked like you might for a while."

"Didn't think I could get past you. It's not quite so painful now."

"Good. It will only get better."

Sylvia chimed in, "When you reach the next level, we can shop for new clothes."

"When will that be?"

"Day after tomorrow. I'll wash your old things this afternoon so you can at least get back into something that fits."

The food had a positive effect. Probably a substantial part of the pain she felt was from a stomach that cried out for nourishment. After lunch they tried to persuade her to nap. She refused. Sylvia started the laundry load with the girl looking over her shoulder.

"Why did you want to be a nun?"

Sylvia sighed, "It's an involved story."

"You don't want to tell me?"

"I'll tell you…let's sit down in the living room."

Delbert was in the den converting their sofa-bed into sleeping configuration.

"Delbert and I were soul-mates from an early age. Delbert is brilliant. He skipped twelfth grade and went straight to university. That left me alone during grade twelve although we got together on holidays. After I graduated from high school, I took a summer job on Salt Spring and planned to get a job in Vancouver in the Fall so we could be together.

"Unfortunately, or perhaps fortunately depending on one's viewpoint, the Air Force decided Delbert would make an excellent test pilot. They offered to train him back east near Toronto."

"Test pilot?"

"Yes, Delbert became Canada's youngest and best jet test pilot."

"Are you pulling my leg?"

"No dear, I will show you some of our memorabilia later. That summer Delbert wasn't around to warn me about my boss. At a logger's convention I had to attend with him, he got me drunk by leading me to think the drink had no alcohol. When I passed out…he raped me."

Sylvia paused to gather herself. "It turned out I was pregnant. I panicked and with no one to turn to, gave myself an abortion. It nearly killed me. I felt disgraced. Didn't know what to do. A priest who visited me in the hospital recommended I talk to a Mother Superior. She comforted me and gave me a way out of my dilemma."

"So it was an escape, not a calling."

"Well…yes. But I found my years as a novitiate fulfilling."

"Why didn't Delbert come rescue you?"

"He tried to for over three years until we finally got together again. I stayed out of communication with him to force him to find another mate who could give him children."

"You couldn't?"

"Can't. The abortion ended that."

"I'm sorry for prying. It must have been hard on you."

Sylvia was teary eyed. "Yes…but you see we can all get through hard times if we persevere."

Cynthia moved closer and hugged Sylvia. They sobbed quietly on each other's shoulder.

Delbert appeared in the doorway, took one look at them and rolled back into the den. They appeared to have bonded. Once again he was proud of Sylvia.

"How were you reunited?"

"Delbert flew a fighter from Comox to Victoria. There was a mid-air collision and he had to crash land the airplane on a golf course to avoid hitting a populated area. He was carried to a Priory in a coma with a broken back and his feet severed off. I worked there as a nurse."

"You nursed him back to life?"

"In a sense, perhaps."

* * *

The next week was hard on Cynthia. Attempts to distract her worked only briefly. They walked in Beacon Hill Park, went to movies, shopped for clothes and coaxed her to play games. When withdrawal pains attacked, Sylvia would hug her and stroke her brow until the worst passed.

They began to see improvement with the increased dosage after a week. Still, she remained unconvinced that it would work and often said she needed a fix. Those were the hardest times. They felt guilty for holding her prisoner. But how else could her life be rescued? It seemed wrong and since she was sleeping better, they relaxed their vigilance.

Then one morning they awoke and she was gone. Delbert discovered she had stolen the cash from his wallet. Rejection left them hurt, helpless and angry.

Chapter 6

After the initial outrage, Delbert's stubborn nature surfaced.

"Grab the methadone jars and let's go after her."

"Do you think we stand a chance of finding her again?"

"Only one way to see."

He headed for the car. Sylvia ran to catch up. She asked where to start as they backed out of the driveway.

"I assume she caught a bus downtown. She probably headed to Johnson Street west of Government. That's the seediest area—most likely to have a pusher on the street."

They patrolled back and forth on the streets in that neighbourhood. No sign of her, not even anyone that looked remotely like a pusher. She was past the time for her pills, not that that would matter if she scored a fix. Or would it? They needed to keep the concentration of methadone up regardless.

Delbert had Sylvia park to let him out. He would search the restaurants and hotels on Johnson Street while Sylvia expanded the search area. He wheeled to the first restaurant, looked inside, then moved on. At a cheap hotel that obviously catered to an hourly trade, he asked the desk clerk if a young blonde girl in a pink top and blue Capri pants had checked in.

"We don't give out info on guests."

Delbert's voice rose. "Tell me now or I'll have the police down here. She's underage and that means sex is rape and you will be abetting the crime."

"Okay, okay, mister. There hasn't been anyone like that here. I swear."

Delbert rolled on down the street. He had no luck place after place. His anger mounted with the futility, but he refused to call it a lost cause. As he worked his way up the opposite side of the street, he confronted a man leaning on a lamppost, smoking a cigarette. Desperate, he asked the man if he had seen a girl that matched Cynthia's description.

The man glanced briefly up the street.

"No."

Delbert followed his glance. There was a row of old office buildings, then a building advertising rooms for rent, another building and finally a restaurant on the corner. He wheeled in that direction. The rooms for rent were above the first story, reached by a dilapidated stairway. As he turned to face it, he noticed the man was gone. *She's here! How can I get up the stairs? I can't contact Sylvia.* He got madder by the minute.

The anger fueled his adrenalin. With the wheelchair braked parallel to the bottom step, he flung himself onto the steps, reached back for the chair and folded it. Then he dragged himself up one step at a time. Every third step, he lifted the chair above him. It took almost fifteen minutes to reach the top, another two to climb back into the chair and wheel to a door with "Manager" hand lettered on a piece of yellowed paper taped next to it.

He knocked and pushed the door open in the face of an old, unshaven man coming to answer it.

"What the hell…?"

"Which room is the blonde girl in?"

"Don't know what you mean?"

Delbert grabbed his arm in a vise grip. "In a pink top and blue pants. Which room? Or do you want to end up in jail?"

The grip hurt. The threat was real. He wilted. "Second door on the left."

"Is it locked?"

"There are no locks. Just a latch on the inside."

Delbert rolled to the door and turned the knob. The door opened. He rolled into the dark room. As his eyes became accustomed to it, he made out the shape of a young girl in a fetal position on the ragged bed. It was Cynthia. He checked her pulse. There was one but it was weak and much slower than normal. Her breathing was shallow. *At least, she's not dead from an overdose. It's bad though. How can I reach Sylvia to get help?* He turned to the manager who had followed him.

"Call an ambulance. I'll pay for it."

The man left. Delbert stroked her brow. She was sweating. *Why did you do this? Couldn't you trust us and work through the pain?* Her desperate plight brought tears to his eyes. He stroked her hair. She could be the daughter he would never have. The man returned.

"They're on the way. Is she a relative?"

"A dear friend."

"I'm sorry. Those damned pushers are the scum of the earth."

"You knew she was in trouble. Why didn't you call the police?"

"They would cut my throat." His sadness and guilt was palpable.

They heard men on the stairs and the manager went out to get them. The first one in checked Cynthia's vital signs.

"She'll live. We need to get her to the hospital though. Are you responsible for her?"

"Yes," Delbert replied, "I'll pay your cost."

The second man said he would get the stretcher.

"Bring a sheet," Delbert said.

The man gave him a quizzical look and nodded. When he returned, they lifted her onto the stretcher.

"Put the sheet over her when you take her out. I want anyone watching to think she is dead."

"Why?"

"So they will stay away from her from now on."

He turned to the manager. "As far as you're concerned, she overdosed. Got it?"

"Yes."

"You better have or you'll get treated the same way the pushers would handle you."

He instructed the driver to take Cynthia to the Jubilee Hospital and gave them his name and address to bill for their service. Then watched them leave with Cynthia under the sheet.

His next challenge was descending the stairs. He braked the wheelchair at the top and pushed his head backwards until he was lying on his back. Then he released the brake and slowly rolled forward dragging his body horizontally. He eased the wheels over the riser. Step after step he crawled down, afraid a runaway would fling him crashing onto the sidewalk or worse, the street. Once the manager could see his plan, he walked down beside him to prevent the back from rising.

On the sidewalk at last, he thanked the manager. Then assumed a dejected pose, head tilted forward. A glance up and down the street revealed no one suspicious but he knew he would be seen. In fact, a man surreptitiously watched from inside a restaurant across the street. When he saw the body carried out, he mentally crossed one more customer off his list. It meant no more than that to him.

Slowly, Delbert made his way to the corner, turned right and moved a block to the next corner. He had to wait until Sylvia found him. It took twenty minutes.

She pulled into a vacant spot halfway down the block. He wheeled to her. From his woeful expression she assumed he had no luck. She ran around to open the door for him.

"We'll find her, dear."

"Get us out of here," was all he said.

She closed his door and put the folded wheelchair in back. *What happened? Is Cynthia dead?* She was afraid to ask. He waited until they were underway.

"She's alive. An ambulance is taking her to the Jubilee. We need to go there."

"Is she conscious?"

"Barely…not really. She got the fix she craved. I hate those bastards!"

Quiet now, they drove to the hospital, each with their own thoughts. He nursed his anger. She wondered how he found her. It didn't surprise her that he did. She was married to a man who never quit until he achieved his goals. He left her with a mixture of awe, love and respect.

* * *

Cynthia had already been admitted to Emergency when they arrived. They identified themselves as her guardians and were told her status, still incoherent but not in immediate danger. The heroin effect would take a few more hours to wear off which would then leave her in severe pain. They asked to be allowed to stay with her.

She was strapped to the bed, her breathing still shallow, her shaking periodically punctuated by a convulsion. They wiped the sweat from her brow. Sylvia held her hand and stroked her arm.

After what seemed hours, she opened her eyes and stared blankly at the ceiling. Long minutes passed before she gained some awareness of her surroundings. She turned slowly to see who held her hand and half-focused on Sylvia. She first thought she was dead and looking at an angel. The pain that wracked her body said otherwise.

When she finally recognized Sylvia and turned to find Delbert as well, she started to cry. Her voice was feeble, her words disjointed.

"Why…don't…you…go…away?"

"Quiet, dear. Try and rest."

"Shit."

Delbert said quietly, "You have finally run into two people as stubborn as you."

She stared at him through the tears. A new wave of pain took her attention away. When it passed, she stared at each of them again. Her addled mind could read the feeling reflected in their teary eyes. She wondered if this was what love is all about. She was afraid to hope so.

Chapter 7

A doctor came by just after eleven. Sylvia stared in surprise.

"Doctor Simpson, good morning."

"Good morning…" He was clearly trying to place her.

"Sylvia Pillage. You treated me about three years ago. I was Sylvia Cairns then."

"The girl with the…" He stopped and looked at Delbert.

"Botched abortion, yes. This is Delbert, my husband."

They shook hands. He turned back to Sylvia.

"You look radiant. Married life agrees with you. Are you related to this girl?"

"We're her guardians now."

He stepped forward to check Cynthia's pulse and eyes. *Is this the child they can't have themselves? Do they know what they are in for with this one?*

"She's coming out of the trance. She will experience considerable pain and craving for more heroin."

"We have her started on methadone," Delbert interjected. "She missed this morning's dosage. Can she still take it?"

"What level is she at?"

"Twenty milligrams."

"I'll have the nurse give her five every half hour to twenty max. That should be tolerated, however, we need to watch for vomiting and get her head up and forward if that happens."

"We'll stay with her."

"Good."

The doctor turned to leave. Sylvia stopped him.

"Doctor, I intended to call you and ask some questions I should have asked three years ago."

He glanced at Delbert, then turned back to her. "I would need to pull your folder and refresh my memory about the details of your case. Would you mind making an appointment with my receptionist? Perhaps an examination would also be in order."

"I'll do that. Thank you."

After he left, they turned their attention back to Cynthia. Obviously in pain, her voice was barely audible when she spoke through her tears.

"I'm...sorry."

Sylvia gave her hand a gentle squeeze. Delbert took Sylvia's left hand in his right, then stretched his left out to Cynthia. She stared at it, then him. Slowly her right hand came out to his. She felt their love, so foreign as to be almost frightening. She knew they would be there for her even though she stole from them, abandoned them.

The next few hours were heart-wrenching for Delbert and Sylvia. Cynthia cycled between violent shaking and trembling tears. They didn't know of the resolve that was building within the girl to hang on to the gift they brought her. She was determined to fight the pain, the craving, the tremors.

By mid-afternoon, her body had accepted the methadone. Doctor Simpson dropped by again and said it was safe to take her home if they wished. Or she could stay in the hospital overnight. They preferred to take her home and indicated they would watch her carefully. Doctor Simpson beckoned Delbert to accompany him to the nurses' station while he signed the release papers.

"The craving will be intense for the next few days. Given any opportunity, she will probably run away again."

"We will mount a twenty-four hour watch this time."

"She won't know for months how lucky she is to have you two on her side. I hope you take a realistic look at your odds for success with her. Any failure will not be your fault."

"I understand. At least now she knows that we're in it for the long haul."

"I admire the two of you and wish you good fortune."

* * *

By five thirty, they were headed home. All three silent in their own thoughts. Cynthia's were still muddled, interrupted by pain. When craving a fix swept over her, she thought of the other two, of the support they offered. She would not let them down. That resolution helped conquer the agony.

Back at the apartment, she did not want to go to bed. She preferred to curl up on the sofa. It was important to keep them in sight. Sylvia cooked dinner. Cynthia was only able to eat a little even though she felt extremely hungry. They didn't press her to take more.

It was after eleven when Cynthia fell into a troubled sleep. Sylvia sat with her while Delbert slept. They had drawn up a schedule which would keep one of them with her at all times. At two in the morning, he relieved Sylvia. Cynthia was in a fitful slumber, periodically interrupted by nightmares.

When she awoke at dawn, Delbert watched her. She was vaguely aware that someone had been with her during the night. It comforted her. Sylvia was up at eight to fix breakfast. Cynthia ate more this time. Delbert upped her methadone dose to twenty-five milligrams. He decided unilaterally to increase it five per day until the craving disappeared.

"You don't have to guard me twenty-four hours a day. I won't run away again."

"We know you don't want to, but the urge may be more than you can fight. We want to help you through that."

"Thank you," she said softly.

The days passed slowly. It hurt to watch the girl in agony. They could tell she struggled valiantly with the craving. As the methadone level increased, the pain and tremors began to subside. After a week, all three could see light at the end of the tunnel. For a few hours, she would almost seem normal. Her sense of humor emerged during these times. Often it led to laughter to Delbert and Sylvia's delight.

Each day further cemented Cynthia's confidence that they would continue to be there for her. She had never felt this before. They became the parents she never had. She could not and would not let them down. Yet a concern that the methadone wouldn't work lingered in the back of her mind.

Chapter 8

Jake Moran's daydream of banging Hank Morgan's daughter Lettie was interrupted by a violent shake.

"Wake up, you lazy son of a bitch. It'll be dark soon. We gotta get going."

"Hell, Hank, I was just getting to the good part."

"Hurry up. Get ready and meet me in the boathouse."

Jake dragged himself off the bed. *Hank would kill me if he knew I lusted after his sixteen-year old daughter. One of these days I'll lay her anyway. She wants it as bad as I do.* He pulled on his boots, grabbed his jacket and headed out.

Hank was topping off the racer's gas tanks when he arrived. Jake unlocked the doors and swung them open.

"Should be a good night. No moon until three in the morning.

At just over twenty knots it would be a three hour run to Squitty Bay on the south end of Lasqueti Island. The sleek powerboat could easily cut the time by a factor of four but they didn't want to draw unnecessary attention. They needed to be there by ten PM, and it was only six thirty when they fired up the engine and backed out of the boathouse.

Hank's daughter was sitting on what passed for lawn between the boathouse and her folk's house. She raised a knee to slide her dress up and reveal her shapely legs. Jake and Hank returned her wave, each with different thoughts running through their heads. When Hank looked away to steer the boat, she pulled her dress up further to give Jake a view he would remember all night.

They took a leisurely course up along the Vancouver Island coastline, no different than hundreds of tourists and sportsmen. From their home at Musgrave's Landing on Salt Spring Island, they headed north out of Sansom Narrows through Stuart Channel until past Gabriola Island, then an open shot up the Strait of Georgia to Lasqueti Island. They slowed to a crawl into the secluded south fork of Squitty Bay and dropped anchor. Their position gave a good view of the shipping lane east of Texada Island. By ten o'clock they had eaten a couple of sandwiches and downed a beer. Now they waited.

Half a dozen ships passed before they spotted the one that counted. It had three lights shining on the starboard side to form an equilateral triangle. Hank raised a powerful flashlight and gave them a short-long-short signal. A single brief flash was returned. Hank started the heavily muffled engine while Jake pulled in the anchor. They swung out to meet and follow the freighter. They used no running lights and kept the speed down to avoid creating too visible a wake.

Soon they were trailing the freighter barely a thousand yards behind. Suddenly there were two brief flashes from the ship. They slowed to a crawl and scanned the water for the buoys that would be bobbing in front of them. Hank spotted the first and steered to it. Jake reached over the side, grabbed the ring on the buoy, dragged it and an attached waterproof package into the boat.

It took more than five minutes to find the second one. For a moment it seemed they must have passed it and were about to double back when Jake saw it off their port side. They retrieved it. Before they moved on, a fifty-pound sack of sugar was tied to each buoy.

The sugar came from a trick learned in the old rum-running days during Prohibition. If the police or coast guard approached, they would drop the rigs overboard. The sugar would drag the drugs and buoy under water. Gradually the sugar would dissolve and allow the buoy to return to the surface. A few hours after passing inspection, they would circle back and pick them up.

Tonight there was little chance of interception at this end of the operation. It was almost pitch black. Barely enough light to navigate, yet more than enough for Hank once he got his bearings. They made a high-speed run home. The only real danger was hitting a deadhead log and the likelihood of that was remote. By one thirty they inched into the boathouse.

Jake closed and locked the doors while Hank unhooked the sugar and buoys. *Two twenty kilo packages of pure heroin*, he thought. *Not a bad night's work.* Jake refueled the boat. Then they each lifted a package onto their shoulder and started up the path from the boathouse. With a flashlight to guide them, they walked past the two houses on up a trail that led into the woods. Half a mile up they turned off the path and crossed over a large rock outcrop. On the far side Hank dropped his package and moved some brush aside to reveal a small cave. They shoved the drugs inside and replaced the brush. Then retraced their steps to the houses.

"C'mon in and have a beer, Jake. That went real smooth tonight."

Jake's hope that Lettie would be up was rewarded. She appeared in a nightgown that left little to the imagination.

"What are you doing up, kid?"

"I woke up when I heard your boat."

"Not likely. She's too quiet when she's throttled back. Now get back to bed."

Lettie left but not without a smirk aimed at Jake. *I would rip off that nightgown and screw you right here on the floor if Hank wasn't in the room.* He wondered how much longer this game could go on. Sooner or later he would catch her alone and satisfy the urge they both felt. For now, he concentrated on his beer.

"That was the easy part, Jake. Tomorrow we divide one package up into five kilos for Victoria and fifteen for Vancouver. On Thursday, the tricky run to the U.S. drop."

"We get paid on delivery. How do the Chinese get paid?"

"The money is slipped onto the freighter in Vancouver for the Canadian package. Don't know how the American side pays them. What do we care anyway? As long as we get ours."

Musgrave's Landing was a small bay on the southwest side of Salt Spring Island. There was no road over the mountains to it. With only a water approach, it made an ideal stopover for smuggling. During Prohibition, the contraband was booze. Now, in the 1960's it was drugs. The market was insatiable and the water pipeline difficult to police, especially for heroin. The Customs folks kept the border crossing checkpoints well patrolled. On the water, they concentrated more on intercepting bales of marijuana. The chance of success was better.

The police learned from experience that it was useless to descend on Musgrave's Landing. Searches always turned up nothing. It was just too easy to hide contraband and it probably never stayed there long anyway. There was no place in the vicinity to stake out the landing and intercept boats coming or going. As a result, the occupants of the two houses tended to be ignored in favor of concentration on other points along the route.

Hank, his wife Madge and Lettie lived in the big farmhouse near the water. Jake and his younger brother Curt lived in a cottage further up the hill. Curt was mentally slow. They never involved him in the operation. His job was to weed the vegetable garden, milk the cow, tend sheep, hunt and fish. A good hunter, he kept both families stocked with venison and frequently brought home a pair of ruffled grouse.

He had a sadistic streak which bothered Madge, however, they had no choice but to put up with him. Lettie encouraged his sadistic pursuits and laughed when he tortured squirrels and crows. He often fished for salmon and cod. When he hooked a worthless dog fish, he cut off its tail and dropped it back in the water. He would laugh as it wiggled the stump of its body, which provided no forward propulsion while it slowly sank to the bottom.

After repackaging the Canadian shipment on Wednesday, the two men waited for dark to slip out on delivery runs. The first drop for Victoria was relatively easy. Their contact hiked to the beach from Cherry Point Road, south of Cowichan Bay. Three men were involved. Two spread out along the beach in each direction to make sure the coast was clear. When satisfied, the third sent three quick flashes in their boat's direction. Hank swooped into the beach and the exchange of heroin for payment was made.

Hank and Jake took the money home and picked up the Vancouver package. This delivery involved a longer, more dangerous trip up through the Gulf Islands and across between Galiano and Valdes Islands, followed by a straight shot to Bowen Island where another land team waited. The drop operation was the same though the stakes were higher. They again used the sugar trick until they reached the beach.

On the return trip the money was placed in a watertight bag and attached to the buoy. These particular drops came off without a hitch. The hard one was yet to come.

Chapter 9

On Thursday evening, fishing gear was stowed in the boat along with the drugs, buoy and sack of sugar. They eased out of the boathouse just after six. Their route would take them down around Victoria, past Metchosin and Sooke staying in Canadian waters. Then they would cross to a desolate stretch of beach west of Port Angeles for the drop. Running lights were a must because of patrol activity in the region, particularly when they crossed into U.S. waters.

They again kept the speed down to avoid suspicion. Things went smoothly until they passed Sooke. Too smooth for Hank's liking. Sure enough, as they started across they spotted a Coast Guard cutter turn toward them. Jake slipped the load overboard on the far side while Hank kept his speed up. They were in U.S. waters when the cutter intercepted them.

The captain ordered them to pull alongside. One of the sailors dropped into the racer without waiting for permission.

"You're in U.S. waters. What's your business?" the captain asked.

"Just want to do a little fishing. Is that illegal on your side?"

"Without a permit, yes."

"Guess I'm not much of a navigator. Didn't know we had crossed the line."

"That looks like a damn powerful boat for fishing."

"Yeah, it's a beauty. Gets up and goes. But it'll idle down for trolling."

"You don't have much light left for fishing."

"The coho often feed for a while at dusk."

The captain gave a noncommittal shrug. The sailor had completed a quick search and signaled the captain that nothing was found.

"We'll lead you back to the boundary. Make sure you stay well north of it in future. Fishing is better close to shore anyway."

"Thank you, Sir"

The sailor climbed back onto the cutter and it began to head north.

"Christ, I hope that sugar doesn't dissolve too quickly," Jake said.

"Shut up and just look naïve, asshole."

At the boundary, the captain waved and turned the cutter back in the direction of Port Angeles. Hank kept straight ahead toward Vancouver Island. Once they were close to shore, they slowed to trolling speed and put out the lines. They suspected the Coast Guard was keeping them under surveillance. When it became too dark to fish, they packed up and made a run into Sooke, out of sight from Port Angeles.

"How the hell are we going to find that buoy now?"

"It's a crap shoot. I took bearings on the shorelines when we dropped it. We need to allow for the tide and start searching as soon as we get a little moonlight."

They waited an hour, then started out again, this time without running lights. If the cutter came back out, they would just have to make a high-speed run into Canadian waters. For two hours they worked back and forth in search of the buoy. It would be back on the surface for sure.

"If we don't find it soon, some lucky bugger will land a fortune."

"Shut up Jake and keep scanning the water on your side."

"It's damn near impossible to see a buoy in this water at night."

"Keep looking."

Another half hour went by. Still nothing. Hank was getting frantic. He didn't want to lose this delivery. It was bad for their reputation. *A loss like this could put us out of business. Worse still, they might send their goons to make sure we're not stiffing them.*

"I saw something!"

"Where?"

"Turn to port and head back."

Hank did. There it was, bobbing in the waves. With a sigh of relief, they retrieved it. As soon as Hank got his bearings, he headed toward the drop point. Would they still be there? When he was offshore from the target, he flashed a light toward shore. One quick flash. There was an answering flash from the beach.

Hank headed in. Within minutes they reached the shore and made the exchange.

"What took you so long? We were about to give up."

"Coast Guard came after us. We need to find a different drop point next time. I can't fool them twice."

"We'll be in touch."

Hank and Jake were on their way again. This time they ran full speed for the Canadian side and didn't stop until they reached home. As they passed Metchosin, they thought they saw what looked like the cutter. He would probably call for help from the Royal Canadian Navy, but they would be safely in the boathouse before anyone could react on this side.

* * *

The three deliveries netted them twelve thousand in Canadian dollars and sixteen in American currency. Hank counted out twenty-five percent of each and passed it to Jake.

"Damn it Hank, I should get more than that. I take as much risk as you."

"I own the boat and farm. And I set up the operation. Stop your bitching. You made seven thousand this week for mainly sitting on your ass."

"You're not counting the work I do on the farm. Still think you're taking advantage of me."

He muttered to himself as he left to go to bed in the cottage. There was a growing nest egg under his floorboards and in the bank in Ganges. But Hank had three times more. *That boat was paid off long ago. Not only that, he's got two women over there, all I got is a dimwit brother.* His plight began to fester.

Chapter 10

Cynthia passed a one-month milestone on methadone. The craving for a fix had passed. Perhaps more important, the three were a family. Delbert and Sylvia delighted in her lively personality and quick wit. It was a mutual attraction. She had never known true parental love and they provided it almost without awareness. Some days she would backtrack along Delbert's exercise route to meet him. Then they would race home. She was fast enough to make a race of it but seldom beat him.

Once she seemed sufficiently stable, they raised the question of schooling.

"I finished grade ten in Campbell River."

"We should get you back in school here."

"Will Victoria High accept her now? The year is three months over." Sylvia questioned.

"I can talk to them and offer to tutor Cynthia to pick up what she's missed. Are you game for that, Cyn?"

She was hesitant. "I don't know if I can fit in. What if kids find out I'm on methadone?"

"There's no reason for them to find out."

"What…if someone pushes me to try drugs?"

They could feel her fear.

"Would you?"

"No! No. But would they ostracize me?"

Delbert thought for a moment.

"We're not naïve enough to think there's no exposure to drugs around the school. I suspect there will be a number of students who also reject the temptation to try them. Only you can decide whether or not you are strong enough to resist peer pressure and find other friends."

There was a long silence before Delbert continued.

"Of course, there's another alternative. You could admit having been addicted and now that you are cured, see how badly it can damage lives."

Finally, Cynthia responded, "I don't know if I'm strong enough for that yet. The challenge of steering kids away from drugs appeals to me. But what if I'm just ridiculed?"

Sylvia interjected, "They're not friends if they do that. I know what you mean though. Why don't you think about it for a few days? We won't force you to risk your recovery. Perhaps you could make an inquiry about getting her into grade eleven in the meantime, Delbert?"

"Sure. Sylvia's right. It's your decision. We would want you to feel comfortable with it."

In bed that night, Sylvia whispered, "Do you think she will go back?"

"To school or to drugs?"

"Both."

"She's a very smart girl. I think the lesson has been learned and her chance of a relapse diminishes with each new week. As for school, it would be a shame not to continue her education, at least through high school."

"Well, it's in her hands now."

Sylvia moved next to him and enticed them both to begin the caresses that inevitably led to sexual pleasures they often enjoyed.

* * *

In the morning, Delbert telephoned the Campbell River High School and requested a copy of Cynthia's grade ten transcript. He had to convince them they were now her guardians. Eventually they agreed to mail a copy.

The three of them drove over to Vic High. Delbert offered to go in alone and talk to the principal.

"We should all go in," Cynthia said. Delbert and Sylvia exchanged glances as they set off.

It took some talking to get an audience with the principal. After introductions, Delbert explained that Cynthia had come to live with them from Campbell River and they wanted to know if she could enter the eleventh grade even though she had missed three months.

"Missed? You mean she hasn't attended school this Fall?"

"Right. She's been ill. I'm having her last year's grades sent down."

Cynthia spoke up. "I was addicted to heroin last summer and am now cured."

The outburst shocked her new parents. The principal first studied her, then them. He seemed to weigh the situation.

"Frankly, we have had little success with addiction. However, I've never had a student make as bold a statement as you just did. I would be a damned poor principal if I turned you away. If your grades are reasonable, we will welcome you."

"Thank you," Cynthia said before Delbert could open his mouth.

"It will be a challenge to make up for three missed months."

"I can tutor her to the extent she wants," Delbert replied.

"Well, let's see the grades when they arrive."

Sylvia broke their silence on the way home.

"You surprised me, Cyn, when you blurted out your situation."

"Me too," Delbert added.

"I thought about it a lot last night and decided the best solution is to face it head on."

Sylvia wiped a tear from her eye as she drove. "That's what makes you so precious to us."

Delbert leaned forward and patted Cynthia on the shoulder. Their emotion was infectious. She felt both warmth and pride.

Chapter 11

It was no surprise to find Cynthia's grades were good, better than good. They placed her in the top tenth of the class. The Vic High principal was pleased. He wanted to see a success story amongst students who had fallen victim to drugs. With careful parenting and helpful teachers, it seemed possible in this case.

Cynthia was introduced to her new home room class as a student who just arrived from Campbell River. The teacher asked the class to welcome her and show her where they were in each subject. Cynthia was given a set of textbooks in use for the year. It didn't take long to identify how much of each book had been covered.

By taking a few books home each night, she was able to let Delbert see what she missed. He read those chapters before going to bed. One reading was all he required. Then, when Cynthia was receptive, he tutored her on the missed material. He concentrated on important topics and screened out the chaff inevitably added to each textbook. She turned into an enthusiastic learner. Within a month, it appeared she had recovered the lost ground.

During their bedroom conversation one evening, Delbert said, "You know, I really enjoyed teaching Cynthia this past month. Maybe I should try to teach or tutor at the college. I need more to do now, and it would give us some additional income."

"We do pretty well on your pension, dear."

"Yes, but it feels like I'm being paid to do nothing."

"You're paid for what you did, not what you're doing."

"Technically, yes. You know what I mean. I have to get on with my life."

Sylvia sighed. "I do know what you mean. You need projects to work on. Actually, now that you've become so darned independent, I've felt some desire to nurse again. The Jubilee could probably use another nurse's aide."

"Okay, we've both a little job searching to do."

* * *

Delbert typed up a short resume. He thought his Engineering Physics degree, with the top honors received, looked good. His experience as a jet test pilot might not carry much weight. Since he had no formal teacher's training, he pointed out his work in developing flight training material and the actual training he carried out.

Then he called Dean Calder, Dan Martin and Mike Medane at UBC to ask if he could use them as references. All three agreed immediately. They were glad to hear from him. The dean wanted to know what he had in mind.

"I intend to talk to the people at Vic College to see if there's any possibility of substituting for professors or tutoring, anything like that."

"Good luck with it, Delbert. They stand to benefit greatly from exposure to your talents."

"Thank you."

* * *

On Thursday, Sylvia drove them to the college. They found their way to the Administration Building. Delbert introduced himself to the receptionist.

"Oh, Mr. Pillage. Dean Farquhar told me to watch out for you and bring you to him when you showed up."

What? He didn't know I was coming... Dean Calder must have talked to him.

The timing was good. Farquhar was able to meet with him.

"Mr. Pillage, may I call you Delbert?"

"Please."

"Well Delbert, I had an interesting call from Dean Calder yesterday. Told me all about you and all the things you've accomplished in a remarkably short number of years. Said I'd be a fool not to get you involved with our college."

Delbert was embarrassed. "He supported me for most of those years. I'm certainly indebted to him. He's a great man. I want you to know I didn't ask him to call you though."

"I know that. Been scratching my head ever since he called. Do you remember any of your Physics 101 material?"

"All of it."

The dean pondered, almost seemed to weigh his thoughts.

"Given your lack of lecture experience, this is risky but— one of our professors wants to resign and raise a family. I've asked her to stay until I can locate a replacement and until now the search has not borne fruit. It's hard to find anyone in the middle of a year."

Delbert watched him, wondering if he would take the plunge.

"Do you think you could get up to speed and take over her two classes after the Christmas break?"

"I would have to take a quick look at the curriculum and textbooks to see what changes have been introduced in the last few years. But yes, I can do it."

"It involves two lectures three times a week."

"I can handle that."

"That's what Dean Calder said. Professor Medane told me my biggest problem would be keeping up with you."

He chuckled. Delbert laughed.

"Okay, I'll introduce you to Jean Conley. She can bring you up to speed on what she's covered so far. Don't mean to question your ability, however, it seems prudent to consider the second term probationary in case we both decide it won't work out."

"Fine. Thank you."

The dean asked his secretary to find out if Conley was at the college and if so, could they meet with her? She was. They did. Jean Conley turned out to be friendly, grateful that a replacement was found and able to spend as much time with Delbert as needed.

Delbert left with a copy of the curriculum and textbook on his lap to search for Sylvia. When she saw him, she got up from the bench where she had watched two men engrossed in a heated tennis match.

"Sorry you had to wait so long."

"That's fine. The grounds are beautiful here. I walked around for a while, then parked here to watch the tennis."

She could tell he was excited. "They offered me a job teaching two Physics classes starting after Christmas."

"Great. That was quick."

"Dean Farquhar expected me. Dean Calder, Dan and Mike put in a good word. Probably the only thing that would have made him consider it."

"They know you well, dear, and would give him an honest recommendation. You'll do them proud. You always do."

"Wish I shared your confidence. It will be a challenge."

Chapter 12

The month of December proved lucrative for Hank and Jake. Two shipments. Both successful. The appetite for heroin seemed to increase before the holiday season. Fog was common this time of year, descending in the late afternoon and not burning off until late in the morning. It was a mixed blessing. They could move undetected, but it left rocks undetected as well.

Once the fog stymied their effort to find two dropped buoys. In a panic they were forced to retreat to Squitty Bay and hole up for the night. Hank spent it alternately cursing their luck and desperately trying to estimate where the tide would take the buoys. Jake fell asleep. Each time he started to snore, Hank kicked him.

Mid-morning Hank decided to venture out. He shook Jake awake. The tide had been ebbing when the drop occurred. The buoys would have drifted out for an hour, more or less sat through the slack tide, and then come back down the channel with the incoming tide.

"Hell, they could be anywhere by now. Might have even washed up on a beach."

A hungry Jake responded, "Maybe we should write them off and head home."

"Leave them? Hell no! We'll hunt all day for them. You take the port side."

Jake sighed and peered into the blanket of fog. At best he could see twenty feet. *This is hopeless but that greedy bastard won't give up a single shipment.*

Hank thought he had the boat positioned fairly close to the freighter's course. He planned to follow it as best he could. Then he realized he needed to follow the tide's course instead. He tried to picture what that would be from his past experience. Everything was stacked against him; fog, tide, time. Soon exposure would have to be added when the fog burned off.

By late morning visibility had improved significantly. Hank speeded up to cover more area in the time remaining.

Jake was edgy. "We're getting too easy to spot. Let's cut our losses and get out of here."

"Shut up until you see a buoy."

By the time the fog finally lifted, he was travelling at full speed in a frantic search pattern. Every few minutes he scanned the horizon for approaching boats. He knew it was reckless but he would take almost any chance to avoid missing a drop.

Suddenly Jake shouted, "Over there! I saw one."

Hank swung the boat around in a violent turn and backed off the throttle. Jake guided him to the spot where he'd glimpsed the buoy and moments later they found and retrieved it. The need for speed was over, He began an expanding circular search pattern. Within ten minutes they found the second one.

"Good eyes, Jake. Knew I brought you along for something. We better hole up in Squitty Bay until the fog rolls in again."

"Shit Hank, I'm starving."

"We'll hide the packages in the brush. Then you can pick some oysters off the beach and shuck them."

"Eat them raw?"

"Sure. Taste best raw. Puts lead in your pencil."

"Got too damned much lead in my pencil already."

Hank laughed. "You can take care of that in Vancouver over Christmas with all this money you're squirreling away."

Jake fell into a silent funk. Twenty-five percent of the take weighed on him more all the time.

By evening they were maneuvering through the fog down the channel. Hank could dead reckon his way home with reasonable safety. There was no concern of interception. But finding the boathouse was a problem. When he thought it must be near, he slowed to a crawl and headed for the beach. Then he turned to creep along the shoreline and try to find a recognizable landmark.

He was about to turn around and look north when he saw the point protecting their little bay. Within minutes, he edged into the boathouse.

"Nobody will be out in this fog. Let's carry the packages up to the house, then get some sleep. In the morning, I'll divide the one for Victoria and Vancouver. You carry the other one up to the cave. We'll make the delivery on time tomorrow night."

All three deliveries went off without a hitch. As long as they could keep off the rocks, fog was their ally. Jake didn't get Christmas in Vancouver as promised. There was a double drop on Christmas Day—four packages. The risk of interception was considered negligible. Hank demanded double payment for delivery. When someone complained that he didn't have to make two trips, he said his cut was a percentage of the final profit—far too small a percentage in fact.

Madge and Lettie felt cheated out of Christmas. When they complained, Hank got mad.

"Quit your bellyaching. We have runs to make. You ought to be thankful we're making a lot of money."

"I never see any of it."

"Quit bitching." He slapped her with the back of his hand. She stumbled backwards.

"Cut that out!" Lettie shouted.

Hank gave her a shove that sent her flying against the wall.

"Get out of my face, both of you," he shouted as he headed into his office and slammed the door.

"I don't know why you put up with him, Mum."

"He has all the money. What can we do? Where can we go?"

Jake heard them shouting. He almost interceded, then thought better of it. *Got to remember which side my bread is buttered on. Burns me up he's got two women that could make both our lives real pleasant and all he does is beat them up.* He was too tired to let the usual frustration build.

Chapter 13

Early in December, Sylvia reminded Delbert that his parents had invited them for Christmas.

"Can we take Cynthia?"

"Sure. They will welcome her too, assuming she wants to go. If she doesn't, we have a problem. If she does, I'll let them know ahead of time."

They broached the subject during dinner. She listened to the proposal but blanched when they mentioned Salt Spring Island.

"They live there?"

"In Fulford Harbour."

She hesitated. "What if we run into Luke?"

There was a pregnant pause before Delbert answered.

"It's not likely. If we do, we'll shield you from him. Tell him we're your guardians now. If he makes a fuss, we can ask him if he prefers to face charges for giving drugs to a minor."

"What if he takes me from you physically?"

"Cal and Mattie Lockhart are friends of mine. They're the police on the island and they would take him out of the picture, if my brother and Dad haven't already done that."

"He's strong."

"So are they. Look Cynthia, you'll be safe with us. But think it over and if you don't want to take the chance, we'll cancel the trip."

"I don't want to spoil your Christmas."

Sylvia piped up, "You'll make this one of our happiest Christmases either way."

"Let's go—if I'm not an imposition on them."

"I've told them about you. They look forward to meeting you. Changing the subject, there's a silly little thing that bothers me. We seem to have homed in on a nickname of Cyn and you are anything but sinful. Is that what you want to be called?"

"Many people use it. Guess I prefer Thia."

"Thia sounds great." Sylvia agreed.

* * *

The two females spent most of a Saturday shopping for presents. The family rule was to keep each under ten dollars. Delbert begged off this excursion claiming his feet couldn't stand such a long time on pavement. The other two groaned and left. When they were out of sight, Delbert wheeled down Oak Bay Avenue to do some secret shopping of his own.

On the twenty-third they took the ferry across. Teresa, Phil and Paul made Cynthia feel part of the family from the outset. She was surprised at Paul's height and size, much taller than his father, he would have towered over a standing Delbert in her estimation. She knew better than to mention that in front of him. He would undoubtedly claim to be just as tall if he still had his feet. It amazed her how he could make fun of his situation and not show regret for what happened.

The next morning Paul said, "We have a family tradition, Thia. I go up the back and find a Christmas tree. Want to help me?"

"Sure."

Teresa made her bundle up and borrow a pair of boots. There was a light snow falling in the calm morning air when they set off. Teresa watched them leave.

"She's a bright and pretty young girl."

Sylvia nodded. "The transformation over the past two months has been miraculous."

"You are the luckiest thing that could have happened to her."

"Paul just seems to keep growing," Delbert interjected. "How's the business working out, Dad?"

Phil glanced at him. "Great. Paul runs the show. I'm the hired help now. We gotta a coupla houses to build after we finish Thompson's. He keeps the costs under control and gives 'em an honest return on their bucks. An' there's no skimpin' on quality. We're gittin' a good reputation here on the island."

"Can't believe you give him that free a rein."

"Yep, I do. He'll be in the construction business long after I'm gone so he needs to make a name for hisself."

Teresa laughed. "You can say that because he is good at the job. Doubt if you could sit still if he were to make a mistake."

In less than two hours, Paul and Cynthia returned. He had an axe in one hand and the base of the tree on the opposite shoulder. She carried the top end of the tree, peering out through the branches. They dropped it in the woodshed and

Paul headed off to get a hammer and saw. Cynthia waved to the others. Her cheeks were red. She beamed.

Teresa opened the door and suggested she come in and warm up. That was flatly rejected.

"We need to get the stand on it."

"Okay, but don't get a chill."

Teresa smiled as she closed the door. Paul was perfectly capable of mounting the stand alone. They watched her help him, holding the tree while he made a fresh cut on the trunk and nailed the pieces of wood which would form the stand.

They carried it in through the front door, made a right turn and soon had it standing in the front end of the living room. Teresa carried in a box of ornaments and tinsel. The women busied themselves decorating the tree while the men talked in the kitchen.

When the tree was nearly finished, Teresa left and returned with a second box.

"I hear people are starting to use electric Christmas tree lights these days. I still prefer candles."

She started passing four-inch candles mounted on small metal wax-catching bases with clamps for attaching them to branches.

"Make sure they will stay upright. We'll light them this evening."

At dusk, when they were lit, the flickering flames reflecting off the ornaments and tinsel gave the tree a magical look. The room had an enchanted ambiance. Cynthia was enthralled. It brought home how much she missed growing up essentially without a family life.

Christmas morning was devoted to opening presents and playing games. Sylvia drove to Ganges to attend mass with her parents. They were invited back to join in the Christmas dinner. Teresa roasted a large turkey with bread stuffing in one end and sausage in the other. Cynthia helped her prepare it and all that went with it. They joked and chatted away in the kitchen while the men talked in the living room.

Delbert asked, "How familiar are you with Luke Adams?"

Both expressions chilled. Paul responded, "He's a no-good troublemaker. Starts a fight nearly every time he drinks. Why?"

"He's Thia's uncle."

"Oh, sorry, I didn't know."

"No need to be sorry. He did his best to ruin her life. We're her guardians now because of him. I only mention it because she's afraid we will run into him, and he will try to take control of her again."

"Probably won't see him outside of a beer parlour."

Phil chimed in, "Take it you're not her legal guardians yet?"

"Legally, no. It would be a long, hard process to gain legal guardianship, especially if her parents decided to fight us."

"Well, Luke's a mean bugger but he's not as strong as he thinks. We can handle him if the need arises."

"Thanks, Paul. Hopefully it won't."

Delbert didn't share his misgiving that someday there would be a confrontation.

Chapter 14

The three returned to Victoria on the second day after Christmas, each with fond memories of family camaraderie. Delbert was anxious to get started at the college and a little apprehensive as well. He had his own idea of how Physics should be taught. Would they let him use his own technique? He was confident the students would learn more if only the dean has patience to see the results.

On the first Monday morning of the new year, he wheeled to the front of a full classroom. They watched him, surprised.

"Professor Conley is taking time off to start a family so I will take over for the rest of the year. I'm Delbert Pillage. It's a strange name and I've heard every possible way it could be debased while growing up. You're welcome to have fun with it on your own time. Now I want to hear each of your names."

He pointed to the first student. They went back and forth along the rows identifying themselves. Then he continued.

"This course will not be taught in the traditional manner in which a lecturer enters, talks to the blackboard for an hour filling it with scribbling which you all feverishly copy down, errors and all, then leaves. As you can see, I can't follow in those footsteps."

This generated a smattering of very tentative chuckles.

"You are allowed to laugh—that was a joke. In truth, if I were to write notes on the board, it would have to be in a very small font along a band across the bottom of this expanse. That won't happen. I want you to enjoy Physics and to see how it can be useful to you in real life. You can't do that writing notes for an hour. I want you to participate in each day's lesson and will tell you when to write something down."

Curious now, students wondered where he was headed. One asked how they would know what to study for exams.

"Good question, Charlie, I will hand out a summarized set of notes a week prior to exams, pointing out what you should understand and where you can find elaboration in the textbook. If you learn as we go, it will simply be a refresher. Now, write this down. 'Page 97 to 101'. Those are the text pages for our next class. Read at least the first two, they contain the meat."

After writing down the pages, a number of students started thumbing to them in the textbook.

"Eyes back here please. John, Sally, Eva and Jerry. One of you will describe the concept to the class and the rest of us will chime in as needed to keep you on the straight and narrow. Jason, Lynn and Edith, you are responsible for problem 3 on page 101 and will write out your solution in front of the class. Sam, Tom T. and Alex, you have problem 5. You can collaborate if you like. All of you, think of ways this quote law unquote applies to our lives. Any questions?"

Silence. Students looked at each other as they tried to decide if they liked this approach.

"Okay, then. One other thing. You could skip classes, study the textbook and perhaps pass the exams. However, I will keep track of attendance and your participation in class and, being only human, will probably favor you accordingly when marking papers."

He laughed and half the class followed.

"I have been blessed and at times cursed with an unusual memory. To prove your attendance will be monitored, I want you to select up to six students who will deliberately show up five minutes late for our next class. When they arrive I will have written their names on the board. Doesn't matter where you each sit. Now, the rest of the hour is yours. You can read the pages, talk about anything or go have coffee."

They watched him wheel out. As soon as the door closed, the conversations began.

Delbert repeated the same introduction with the second class.

* * *

On Wednesday, Delbert rolled into the first class, scanned around the room and immediately wrote five names on the board. There were gasps when the five students walked in.

He asked each of the assigned groups who wanted to teach their part of the lesson or problem. He had to encourage them to step forward but after twenty minutes he had an energetic dialog underway between students. A few laughs brought relaxation. By the end of the hour, he sensed enthusiasm.

He knew it would take time for all the students to gain confidence in his method. Probably some would remain apprehensive until after the mid-term exams. Yet he was confident they would learn more thoroughly and retain what they learned longer. *If only the Dean doesn't decide to monitor my classes and force me back to formal lectures.*

Within three weeks, Delbert could see the system met his expectations. Students obviously enjoyed his classes. Lively dialog flowed in both directions. Reluctance to put material on the board faded away when they realized there was no threat involved. The subject came to life for them. At one point, a student questioned whether or not they were learning enough for the exams since classes were so much fun.

"Mabel, think of it this way. In three weeks we have covered forty pages of text. That's right on schedule. Can you find anything significant in those pages that you don't understand? In fact, let's make that an assignment. Before Monday, find time to thumb through those pages and jot down anything you don't understand on a scrap of paper. Toss them with your name on my desk."

On Monday, there were three sheets each with one topic. Delbert reviewed the topics privately with them. *Is this a meaningful test of my method?*

Chapter 15

Cynthia made friends quickly. Her looks, wit and cheery outlook led to popularity with both genders. She could easily spot students who had tried drugs. At first she simply shied away from them. It became harder as she watched the progression she knew so well. Whenever a student suddenly disappeared from school it tore at her heart. She made an appointment to talk to the principal at the end of January.

"What do you wish to discuss, Cynthia?"

"I would like five minutes at the end of the next school assembly to talk about the drug threat."

"Are you sure you want to do that?"

"Yes Sir. I've thought about it a lot."

He looked at her long and hard. It could be helpful, but will other students accept what she says or write her off as a little miss goody-goody.

"Your classmates might take offense…think you are our shill."

"I don't think so."

He paused longer. There is risk involved—to her and the school. Benefits always involve risk.

"Okay, we'll give you five minutes on Friday afternoon."

* * *

Cynthia walked straight to the microphone. She looked small on the big stage. There was some applause, a few catcalls. She waited for silence.

"I'm a drug addict! Every morning I take eighty-five milligrams of methadone. If I ever quit, I will be back on heroin within a week. I will probably have to take the methadone for the rest of my life."

There was a shocked silence in the auditorium.

"How did it happen? The same way it usually does. A persuasive guy approaches you, perhaps at a party or outside the store down the street. You've seen these guys. He strikes up a conversation, maybe flirts with you, eventually asks if you would like to experience a thrill beyond your wildest dreams. You say you shouldn't. He says come on, it's perfectly safe. I'll do it with you to prove it.

"You're curious. You think one time won't hurt. So you watch him give himself a shot and then let him do the same to you. Only you don't know his shot is just sugar and water. And you do get an unbelievable thrill. When it's over he says see, wasn't that great? You admit it was. A day later, he catches you again and offers a second shot. You've had a mild longing to do it again, so you say yes.

"You may not realize it. You are already hooked. The craving is stronger, and you feel depressed. You begin to look for him. The third shot seals the deal. Now you need a fix. Only now he tells you that these shots are expensive. He can't keep on giving them for nothing. How much? Twenty dollars. You spend your allowance, start borrowing from friends.

"Pretty soon you are stealing money from your parents, even some of your mother's jewelry that she seldom wears and might not miss for a while. He shows you where you can fence stolen merchandise. You shoplift. Guys steal cars. Anything for a fix. And the price goes up."

So did the intensity and volume of her voice.

"You can't find the money and beg him to tide you over. If you are an attractive girl, he says he will give you a fix for sex. You don't want to, but you have no choice."

Tears began to trickle down her cheeks. Students hardly dared to breathe. Some of the teachers looked at the principal thinking he should stop this. The principal stared at Cynthia without moving.

"The next time he wants you to have sex with a friend of his who will pay for it. You realize you are now a prostitute. It doesn't matter anymore. You leave school, can't face your parents. He gives you a rented room downtown to use. You take anyone he sends. Imagine the dirtiest, fattest, ugliest man you can. Would you have sex with him? Yes, you would! He could even slap you around if he wanted!"

The tears were flowing freely now. Every eye stared at her. She continued in a quieter voice still easily heard throughout the dead silent auditorium.

"I was one in a thousand who was lucky enough to be rescued by two incredible people. Even when I stole from them and ran away, they hunted me down and forced me into the methadone program. One in a thousand. No ten…no, one in a hundred thousand. Most addicts are dead within five years."

Sadder now…

"It all starts with one shot…one thrill. I know some of you have tried it. Some are gone from school. Don't think for a moment their family just moved away. When a pusher approaches you, say no...just say no! Band together with other classmates and confront the pushers. Drive them away by threatening to turn them in. Take a camera and photograph them. They will disappear for good. But mainly, just say no...please...just say... no...please..."

Her voice trailed off in the silent room. No one moved. Minutes passed. She looked even smaller, sobbing, so vulnerable. Then a classmate stood up, walked to the stage and hugged Cynthia. Then another and another. A dozen students stood in a group hug on the stage. The principal stepped in from the wing, his voice thick with emotion.

"In all my years with students I have never witnessed the bravery we saw just now."

There were tears in his eyes.

"Take what Cynthia said to heart. Make our school drug-free. Any of you who have tried drugs, it's not too late to back out. Come and see me. I can get you help. We want you with us, not spiraling down the hellish road Cynthia described. Now, please return to your homerooms and discuss what you heard amongst yourselves or involve your teachers if you like. Thank you."

A shocked crowd of students quietly filed out leaving Cynthia and her classmates standing alone on the stage. A smattering of students remained scattered about the hall. Some cried. It dawned on the principal that they were some who had tried drugs.

Cynthia saw them too. She led her group to the nearest and hugged her. Then while classmates held the girl, Cynthia moved on to the next. The principal watched them gather all of the stragglers and move outside. He followed them and stood on the front steps.

Outside other students swelled their ranks into what became a little army moving down the street to where a man leaned against a lamppost. He stiffened at their approach. A tall boy the principal recognized as a senior class leader moved out in front. He told the pusher to beat it and never come back or they would pass a photograph of him to the police. The pusher thought of brazening it out, but he saw some of his marks in the crowd. They could finger him. He turned and ran for his car a block away.

The army turned toward the store. A man in front saw what happened and hurried away. Elated with their success, the crowd returned to the school and separated into their respective classrooms.

The principal retreated to his office. *She's worked a miracle! Thank God she came to us.* He called Sylvia at home and described what happened.

"I think she's alright. Her classmates have bonded with her even stronger than before. However, you might want to come and pick her up."

"I'll come right away."

"I can't stress enough how brave she was to take that chance and bare her soul to the school. She is a wonderful girl."

"We know."

Sylvia related what happened to Delbert and together they headed to school. They found her in her homeroom. Others in her class were still with her, along with the teacher. When she saw Sylvia, she ran and hugged her. Delbert sat beside them.

"I feel like standing up and hugging you too," he said.

"Maybe you can, Dad, it's a day for miracles. My friends stuck with me."

She had never called him Dad before. Less than ten years older than her, still it filled him with pride, left a constriction in his chest and he could only speak with emotion.

"Thia, you are a magnificent girl. Sylvia and I are so proud of you!"

On the way home, Cynthia asked, "Do you think it did any good or will they forget all about it in a couple of days?"

Sylvia answered, "From what was said and what I saw, I think it will have a lasting effect. If it does nothing more than save one life, was it worth it?"

"Yes, even one life would be great."

"Chances are it will save many lives, especially if it changes the school culture." Cynthia smiled at her words.

Chapter 16

Mid-January Jake came home from a delivery to find Curt grinning from ear to ear.

"What's so funny?"

"Lettie taught me to fug."

"What?"

"Lettie taught me to fug."

"What do you mean?" He knew and his anger neared the boiling point.

"You know." He mimed the in and out thrusting.

Jake grabbed his shirt and slapped him hard across the face. Curt's nose started to bleed.

"You stay away from her! Do you hear me? Stay away!"

He slapped him again. He knew in his heart that his anger was fueled by jealousy. The dumb bastard had accomplished what he had longed to do for half a year now.

"I didn't do anything, Jake. She come here and made me do it. Honest, Jake."

His anger ebbed. "Stay away from her. Don't let her in. If Hank finds out, he'll kill you. Understand?"

"But I like to fug."

"It's fuck. And you won't like it if Hank catches you."

That brought a meek, "'kay, Jake."

Jake tossed and turned all night. He couldn't erase the image of the two having sex on Curt's bed. *She knows I want her as much as she wants it. Why settle for him? Just letting me know if I don't make a move, she'll go with second best? She's goading me.* It never dawned on him that Curt might be able to more than satisfy her lust.

Only two weeks later, Hank came home to find Madge alone.

"Where's Lettie?"

"I think she's over playing with Curt."

Hank crossed to the cottage to call her home. When he walked in, he heard an unmistakable noise coming from the bedroom. He ran in. Curt was on top of Mattie who had her eyes closed and mouth parted in ecstasy. He grabbed Curt's rifle leaning against the wall, swung it with all his might and hit Curt in the back of the neck. The jolt caused the rifle to fire over Hank's shoulder. Lettie screamed.

Hank flung Curt off, grabbed Lettie's wrist and threw her across the room.

"Get home you little slut!"

Jake was on his way back from caching the shipment in the cave. He heard the gunshot, feared the worst and ran down the hill.

The shot brought Madge out too. She collided with a naked Lettie and immediately realized what happened. She took Lettie back in their house to get dressed.

Jake burst in to see Hank leaning over Curt's body. Hank looked up at him.

"He's dead."

"You shot him?"

"No. I hit him with the stock and the gun went off. Didn't mean to kill him."

"You murdered a dumb, defenseless boy."

"He was raping my daughter."

"Like she didn't want it."

"Back off Jake. He got what he deserved."

"Bull shit. She led him on and you know it. He didn't have the brains to know it was wrong."

"That's my daughter you're talking about."

"That's my brother lying there."

They paused. "Look, Jake, I'm sorry. Lost my temper when I saw them screwing. Really didn't mean to kill him. He did a lot of good for us."

"Get out of here."

* * *

Madge opened the conversation over breakfast. Lettie was afraid to show her face.

"You really did it this time."

"Don't you start in on me. Got enough trouble without you putting in your two cents worth."

"What are you going to do?"

"Don't know yet."

"Is Jake going to the police?"

"We can't let that happen. It'll kill our operation."

"What do you mean 'we'?"

"You stand to lose as much as I do."

They both thought for a minute.

"Frankly, it seems like I don't have much to lose at all. I never see the benefit of what you make. I could probably talk him out of going to the police but what's in it for me?"

"You talk him out of it and I'll give you five thousand in cash. I'd go myself but he and I been at loggerheads lately."

Another minute passed.

"All right, I'll see what I can do. Now you tell Lettie it's safe to come out. Tell her you're not mad at her anymore."

She walked out, crossed the yard and knocked on the door. No answer. She eased the door open. Jake sat at the table, his head in his hands. She closed the door and quietly walked over to him. Placed her hand gently on his shoulder.

"Jake, you okay?"

"He didn't have to kill him."

"What if it was your daughter?"

"Don't know. They were both just trying to find something enjoyable in this God forsaken hell hole."

She gently massaged his shoulders.

"Is that the way you feel too? Bored and frustrated?"

"What the hell do you think?"

"Would it surprise you to learn I feel exactly the same way?"

He turned to look at her. The buttons down the front of her dress were undone to the waist. He couldn't take his eyes off her cleavage.

"You've got him."

"He just slaps me around."

She moved in closer, pulled her dress up, straddled his lap and pulled his face to her breast.

"Jesus, Madge, I've only got so much will power."

"Forget the will and show me the power."

She was undoing his shirt. He started on the rest of her buttons while she tore at his belt.

"What if Hank walks in on us?"

"He won't."

She stood up and pulled him to the bed, her dress fell off on the way. *God, she's got a beautiful body!* On the bed they let loose long pent up passions.

Afterwards, she kissed him.

"That's the kind of sex I dream about."

"Never knew it could be so good."

"We need to find ways to make it happen often."

"Hank will find out sooner or later."

"He's always taking money into town or off setting up drops. Besides he's naïve enough to think I wouldn't dare. He thinks I'm in here talking you out of going to the police over Curt."

"Is that what you came for?"

"It was…until I saw you."

He smiled. "You made a pretty persuasive argument."

"After that sex, I wouldn't mind seeing him hang for murder. Get him off my back and you on it." She laughed and kissed him.

Jake was quiet for a minute. "I thought about it last night. At first I wanted to kill him myself. Then I thought about turning him in. But after all is said and done, the boy's gone. What good would come of bringing the law down on us? It would kill the operation."

"But what do we do with Curt?"

"Dig a grave up the back out of sight and bury him there. No one will ever ask about him."

"Hank would sure like that. Can I tell him that's what you want?

"Sure. And tell him I want thirty-five percent of the take from now on."

"Okay. I better get back to him. Let him think I talked you into it."

They kissed again. She got up and dressed, straightened her hair and left. Jake watched her go from his bed, then decided he better get dressed in case Hank stormed over. He knew the additional ten percent would cause a fuss. *Well, Curt, seems like you did me one last great favor.*

Chapter 17

With a week under his belt at the college and Cynthia's experience fresh in his mind, Delbert was plagued by the thought that more should be done to curtail drug exposure. On Tuesday, he persuaded Sylvia to drive them to the main police station. He asked to talk to someone concerned with drug trafficking. That turned out to be Detective Jesse Thompson.

"Good morning, folks. I'm Jesse. How can I help you?"

"I'm Delbert Pillage and this is my wife, Sylvia."

They nodded and smiled at each other. The men shook hands.

"For the last few months, we've gone through the trials of rescuing an addicted teenager. We know the pushers target schools and can't help wondering if more can be done to dry up the drug flow."

Jesse sighed. "It's a constant battle just to prevent the situation from worsening."

"How do the drugs get here?"

"Are you talking hard drugs—as opposed to marijuana?"

"Yes. Heroin specifically."

"That's the hardest to interdict. It can be shipped in small packages. Around here we know it comes in by sea. Trouble is, it's darned hard to catch smugglers. We have patrol boats out but they seem to know when we're coming and every boat we search comes up clean."

"What about air patrols?"

Sylvia turned to Delbert, an "Oh no" look on her face.

"Similar problem. You can hear an airplane before it gets close enough to spot them."

"So you see no way to reduce the flow?"

"We battle it best we can with the resources available. Stop it? Won't happen."

"I see. Well, thanks for your time."

As they left, Sylvia fervently hoped the conversation didn't sound like a challenge to Delbert. It was one windmill she didn't want him to tilt.

Delbert was quiet on the trip home. Her concern mounted the longer he meditated. She knew what was coming before he spoke.

"You know, Sylvia, I've had an urge to buy an old airplane and fix it up with hand controls so I could fly it. Thompson's comments make me think there's a more meaningful avenue to pursue."

Hopes dashed. "What do you mean?"

"I think I can design a light airplane that is almost silent. It could be useful for drug interdiction."

"Who would build it?"

"Good question. I'll think about it anyway."

She knew a seed planted by Delbert invariably grew. She might as well resign herself to this one.

* * *

A week passed with no mention of a silent airplane. That didn't lull Sylvia to think it forgotten. The routine of driving him to college three days a week weighed on his mind. At breakfast he brought up the subject.

"It bugs me that you need to drive me to the college and come back to pick me up later. It wastes a lot of your time three days a week."

"I don't mind."

"I do. We should look for a place nearer the college so I can wheel myself to work."

"We can if you want. Perhaps we could find a little bigger place to give Cynthia more space and separation."

"And a shop."

Sylvia cringed inside. The seed had germinated. Its plant just popped out of the ground.

On the weekend, they enquired at a local real estate office. The agent indicated a lot of rental houses were currently available. He thumbed through his list with their wishes in mind.

"Two might fit the bill. How about I take you out to look at them?"

"With Delbert's wheelchair, it might be easier for us to drive you."

The first house on Cochrane Street was just two and a half blocks from the college. Although it was bigger than necessary, it had a detached double garage which Delbert thought would make a good shop. The second house was six blocks further away. It appeared somewhat run down. Even though more expensive, the first house made decision easy. They took one more look and told the agent they would rent it.

The house also excited Cynthia. A full bedroom of her own. And it had a desk along with the usual bedroom furniture. In fact, the whole house was tastefully furnished. None of the quirky pieces often found in rentals. The agent told them it was owned by a dentist who made a point of picking up rental properties as an investment.

It was further from Vic High but only half a block from a major bus route on Richmond Road so she would have no difficulty getting to and from school. And it was closer to Jubilee Hospital which appealed to Sylvia. She would now be free to take a part-time job there. They returned home in high spirits to give notice and plan the move.

The only cloud on Sylvia's horizon was the garage, soon to be a shop. She wondered what Delbert intended to do with it.

Chapter 18

Three mornings a week Delbert wheeled off to college, along Cochrane to Richmond Road, then north to cross Landsowne. That put him on the campus and left a block of walkway to reach the buildings. He became a familiar sight rolling along faster than the walkers. Students referred to him as the wheelchair professor. Those in his classes reported they were never bored.

The house had a den Delbert could call his own. Sylvia noticed he spent a lot of time in there. She tried unsuccessfully to curb her curiosity when she poked her head in to tell him dinner was ready. He worked at a table he could wheel right up to, a table now covered with sketches of what appeared to be an airplane. A very strange shape but it had wings and a tail.

"What are you working on, dear?"

"It's a super quiet patrol aircraft designed to be flown in a wheelchair."

"I was afraid of that."

"You know I can't sit by when something could be done to avoid what Thia went through."

"Drug runners must be vicious, not people you should get mixed up with."

"My plan would be to observe them from a distance and let the authorities know how to catch them. It wouldn't be dangerous."

"It would if they figure out what you're doing and come after you."

"Perhaps. Don't know if I can come up with a design that works anyway. But if I do it would give me a chance to fly again."

"Obviously I can't dissuade you." She looked over his shoulder. "That's the weirdest airplane I've ever seen."

Delbert laughed. He was about to describe the design when the phone rang. Sylvia answered. She covered the mouthpiece as she handed it to him.

"Chuck Lansbury," she whispered.

"Chuck! How are you?"

"Great. You?"

"Fine. Where are you?"

"Here in Victoria with a couple of days off. Can we get together and catch up? I heard by the grape vine that you're a high falooting professor now."

"The professor part is right. Don't know how falooting I am."

He covered the mouthpiece while Chuck laughed and whispered to Sylvia, "Dinner?" She nodded.

"Chuck, how about dropping by for dinner tonight?"

"Sure it's no trouble for Sylvia?"

"She suggested it," he lied. "Do you have our Cochrane Street address?"

Chuck didn't. After Delbert dictated it, he suggested a three o'clock rendezvous to give them some time before dinner. Chuck agreed and thanked him.

* * *

The doorbell rang five minutes early. Sylvia answered it and welcomed Chuck.

"Sylvia, you're one of those rare creatures that always looks even more stunning than memory serves."

"Hi Chuck. Flattery is not needed. I plan to feed you anyway. Delbert's in his den."

The two friends shook hands, genuinely glad to see each other. Sylvia marveled at how completely Delbert had forgiven Chuck for causing the crash that left him paralyzed.

For half an hour, they filled each other in on recent events in their lives. Chuck now had his lopsided Pillager wings and "Bentwing" Carson wanted him to join the training corps.

"How is Bentwing?"

"Crusty as ever. Still talks about you and bemoans your loss. Makes me feel like a shit all over again."

Delbert laughed. "His loss was my gain."

The talk turned to Delbert's job at the college and how much he enjoyed it.

"These kids really want to learn. Not like all you headstrong pilots who think you know everything already."

This time Chuck laughed and nodded.

"We are in the process of adopting a teenage girl. You'll meet her at dinner. She's in grade eleven and a real joy."

"What possessed you to do that?"

"She was abandoned by her parents. We took her in. Thia's a great kid, smart, pretty, great sense of humor. You'll like her. Everyone does."

"Well, great. There's never a dull moment in your life. You look very fit. What do you do for exercise?"

"Three days a week, I roll to school and back. I've set up an eight-kilometer track on the local streets for the other four days."

"You and your tracks."

"And I have that exercise machine," he added pointing.

"How does that work?"

"I fasten my stumps in those stirrups and pedal the other end with my hands. It exercises my legs. Keeps the circulation up in them."

Chuck shook his head in amazement. He glanced at the table covered with sketches.

"What's all that?"

"Don't laugh. I'm designing an airplane I can fly."

"Somehow that doesn't surprise me. Let's see it."

Delbert pulled two sheets from the table, side and frontal views.

"Geez, Delbert, you think you can get Mach two out of this crate?"

"I'll be happy if it reaches a hundred knots. It's a flying boat for patrolling the islands."

"Patrolling for what?"

"Drug runners."

"Should have known you'd have a new quest. I've heard those guys run some high-powered speed boats. Might even outrun your machine."

"Perhaps, but that's not the point. This airplane is designed to be quiet—so quiet they won't hear it coming. Its purpose is just to figure out where they are and what they're up to, then alert the authorities. I'm not mounting guns on it," he chuckled.

"Tell me what I'm looking at."

"Okay. From the bottom up. Its base is a fourteen foot Boston Whaler with a flat honeycomb deck bonded onto it. A lightweight VW engine sits above that in the middle. The engine drives two fifty-four-inch diameter industrial ducted fans which take in air up here and blow it out through these cones.

"The wing has a single flap high lift airfoil inboard and what I call flaperons outboard of this fence. The fence also supports the sponson. The engine fan pulls air through the center, blows it over the engine and mixes it with the exhaust coming out of the muffler. Then it's all ducted up and blown along the wing leading edges. The heat provides anti-icing and the wing muffles the sound. The engine compartment is also soundproofed so there won't be any engine noise.

"The gas tank is up here in the body behind the wing to gravity feed the engine. The controls will be fly by wire and all hand operated. There are heavy duty truck batteries under the engine and up forward. This gadget behind the transom is a water jet. It takes water up through an electric pump which pushes it to the outlet pipe. The whole thing is steerable and retracts in flight. It will let me maneuver the plane like a boat on the water and help with acceleration during takeoff. That's it in a nutshell.

"Oh, wait a minute. I forgot the best part. The left side doesn't have a seat. The side window flips up. The side wall behind the window drops down to form a ramp to the dock. I wheel up the ramp into the airplane, turn and roll forward to the controls, then lock my wheels to the deck. There's two seats on the co-pilot side."

Chuck laughed. "Should have known. Don't know what to say. Looks crazy but it makes sense. Lot of new ideas there. Won't the hull be heavy?"

"That's why I chose a Boston Whaler. It's incredibly light and strong with tremendous floatation buoyancy. According to my calculations, it will easily support the plane. I'm thinking of injecting Styrofoam in place of the air space. It will be unsinkable as long as I keep it right side up."

"Who's going to build it?"

"That's the big question. A lot of components can be bought, new or used. The frame, ducting, skin, wings and flaps are a real problem."

They were interrupted by Cynthia's entry.

"Hi Dad. Oh, excuse me. Didn't know you had company."

"Thia, this is Chuck Lansbury, an old flying buddy. Chuck, meet our daughter Cynthia."

"Hi, Mr. Lansbury."

"Call me Chuck, Cynthia. You're as pretty as Delbert claimed."

"Pretty plain next to Mum."

"Granted, she's tough competition. Delbert seems to have a way of surrounding himself with beautiful women."

Chapter 19

Dinner was accompanied with spirited conversation and many laughs. While Sylvia and Cynthia washed dishes, Chuck brought up the airplane again.

"You know, it strikes me there's a lot of fiberglass work involved in your project."

"That's right. Seems like except for wing spars and skeleton frame, the skins, fairings, ducts and flight controls should all be fiberglass, assuming it can be kept light enough."

"Did you know my old man built fiberglass boats for over ten years? He's picked up a lot of know-how."

"Maybe he could give me some professional advice."

"I think so. Want me to ask him to come over and look at what you've got?"

"Could he? That would be great. Where is he now?"

"Over in Esquimalt."

"Right here in town?"

"Yeah, he has a little shop behind the house. How be I bring him over tomorrow to meet you and go over your sketches?"

"Wonderful."

* * *

Chuck's old man turned out to have a name. Max proved quiet next to Chuck's flamboyant extrovert nature which must have come from his mother. A rapid assessment of Max left Delbert convinced he combined a patient, friendly demeanor with a methodical approach to life. After pleasantries were exchanged, Max was anxious to see the sketches. He studied them for some time.

"Chuck said you planned to use fiberglass for skins on the body and wing?"

"That would be my preference because of the shapes involved."

"Lightness must be a lot more important than on boats."

"Yes, every ounce counts."

"Is the wing shape the same all the way along?"

"The inboard section is all one shape and the outboard another."

"But there's no tapering?"

"That's right."

"I can see making molds for wing sections, both webs and skin. Those shapes on the body are another matter. Are you planning to build more than one of these?"

"No."

"In that case, it might be possible to bend pressed paperboard over the frame to get the shape you want. Then lay a fiberglass layer on top of it."

"You mean leave the cardboard in?"

"Oh no, you would pull the fiberglass off and remove the cardboard before fastening the skin to the frames."

"I can see I need someone with your expertise to build this thing."

"Why not me? It looks like fun and I have nothing better to do. And the price is right since my labor comes free."

Delbert was excited. "Really? Max, I almost concluded the project was too much for me but with your help and knowledge it seems possible again."

"Let me jot down my phone number. Give me a call when it's convenient to come over and go into more detail."

"Will do. I teach at the college Monday, Wednesday and Friday mornings. The rest of the time I'm free to work on this. Let me get these sketches turned into dimensioned drawings and then I'll call you."

The rapport developed so quickly by the two men made Chuck smile. *Maybe this is a way to repay Delbert at least in part for keeping me flying after the crash.*

* * *

Delbert still bubbled with enthusiasm at dinner.

"Chuck's father is an expert with fiberglass. He wants to work with me on the airplane."

"That's good, dear." She didn't sound excited.

Cynthia chimed in, "Are you really going to build that weird looking plane? Will it actually fly?"

"There are a lot of if's still. If I can find a Boston Whaler, an engine, industrial fans that would work and a ton of other parts. Not to mention a design that will actually fly, as you put it."

Sylvia liked the idea of him tackling a significant project. *He thrives on that. I just wish the end result didn't involve tangling with smugglers.* She took comfort in the fact that would be far in the future. Or would it?

For the next two weeks, Delbert spent every spare moment in his den. Configuring an airplane was like solving a jigsaw puzzle. Every piece had to fit in the three-dimensional design. The center of gravity had to be precisely located relative to the center of lift of the wings, while remaining balanced over the hull. The airfoil shape must be optimized for low-speed flight. Air inlets and exhausts designed for proper yet quiet airflow. Fans selected to give maximum thrust at all flight speeds without breaking apart.

Once the configuration gelled, he began to produce drawings needed for the fiberglass molds and the metal framework. It was time to invite Max Lansbury over.

* * *

"Since the outer half of your wings tilt up slightly, I think the spars should not be aluminum beams."

"It's called dihedral. What do you suggest?"

"I think we should use a roll of aluminum sheet that runs from wing tip to wing tip. Cut it to shape, drill holes to make it perforated, then layup fiberglass on both sides bonded together through the holes. It would be stronger and probably lighter. Perhaps it should be bolted to an aluminum angle bar running across the inboard wing section to give added strength between wing and body as well as to the sponsons."

"I trust your judgment."

"It'll be easy to make a mold for the webs with holes located to provide the muffling effect. I suggest making the wing skin in two pieces, one containing the leading edge over the top to the trailing edge, the other providing the bottom surface which would be put on last."

"Sounds good, Max. We can run wires and tubes before bonding the bottom on."

"Yep. Flaps would be the same. Leading edge and top one piece, mold in the webs and then stick on the bottom."

"So you don't see any roadblocks with the wings?"

"Nope. There's details to work out relative to hanging the flaps but no showstoppers I can see."

"I'm excited! The next step is to find the big items—Whaler, engine and fans. If we can get them, we can start building molds and pieces."

"We need a full-size drawing of your airfoils. Then I can make a mold or two."

"I'll get them to you tomorrow."

Chapter 20

Hank and Jake dug the grave in a secluded little clearing almost a mile up from the beach. Deep enough to prevent animals from smelling and rooting around in the site. They carried Curt's body up and buried him, then packed the dirt down and made sure neither a mound nor depression would give the location away.

Curt's death bothered Jake more than he expected. He had enjoyed the simple things life presented him in a way often found with mentally challenged children. Only his sadistic streak clouded Jake's memory of him. A week after the burial, Jake casually made his way to the grave site. His excuse was to check on it. His reason was to quietly pay his respects to his brother.

He stopped short when he spotted an arrangement of daisies on the grave. *Who put them there? Had to be Lettie. Certainly not Hank or Madge.* The fleeting shock that an outsider had found it seemed ridiculous on reflection. No one walked over the mountain to reach their farm. He threw the flowers into the brush and returned home, jealous of Curt's continued influence on Lettie.

She was feeding the chickens when he found her.

"For Christ's sake quit putting flowers on Curt's grave. We need it to disappear before someone else finds it."

"I don't know what you're talking about."

"Don't give me that crap. It had to be you."

She turned away to collect eggs. He stared at her. The way her dress revealed her shape excited him, almost lured him into the chicken house after her. That would be too dangerous. He turned to look for Hank. She watched him walk down the slope, a mocking smile on her face.

"Hank, one of your women put flowers on that grave. Lettie claims it wasn't her, but I don't believe it. You better get them to leave it alone. Let things grow over it."

"I'll talk to them. After I run Lettie over to school in the morning, I'm heading into Sydney to set up the next drop. Need anything?"

"Pick up a couple of salt licks for the animals and we're low on grain for the chickens."

* * *

Madge watched Hank through the binoculars. As soon as he dropped Lettie off and headed for Sydney, she called Jake.

"He's past Swartz Bay by now."

Within minutes their clothes formed a path on the floor to the bedroom. The thought crossed Jake's mind that this wasn't such a hell hole after all. He must remember to continue the complaints with Hank to avoid suspicion. Then he forgot everything but Madge.

By the time Hank returned, Jake was repairing a fence around one of the two fields. He whistled as he worked until Hank showed up.

"There's a drop scheduled for Wednesday."

"Okay. We need to get the shearing set up. Luke gets busy in the Spring. Need to get him booked early."

"I'll call him next time I'm in town. You mind picking Lettie up this afternoon?"

"No. Fine."

* * *

Lettie smiled when Jake showed up at Cowichan Bay in the racer. She dropped her books on the seat and sat on the coaming across from him. He told her to hang on as he turned for home. She deliberately let the wind blow her dress up and smiled again as his eyes roved over her legs. She crossed behind him, pressed her breasts against his shoulder and leaned down close to his ear.

"Sure you want to go straight home?"

"You know damn well that I don't. Hank may be watching so back off."

She sat down and pouted, "You're no fun."

It's a good thing I had that session with Madge this morning. This would be too hard to resist without that.

After a moment, she continued, "You don't worry about him when you screw Mum."

Jake blanched. "What are you talking about?"

His reaction confirmed her suspicion.

"Come on Jake, I'm not blind."

"You talk nonsense so knock it off."

"I know exactly what I'm talking about—and so do you."

Further conversation was cut short as they entered the bay. Jake trembled slightly while he tied the boat up. This was not a good turn of events. Lettie laughed as she brushed past him and headed for the house. He couldn't trust her to keep quiet.

The run on Wednesday and deliveries on Thursday and Friday went smoothly. On Saturday Hank headed back to Sydney again. Jake was frustrated by Lettie's presence. She knew it and teased him.

"What's the matter, Jake? Am I in the way?"

He headed up the hill to get away. Frustration mingled with anger made him hurl a rock at a cluster of sheep that scattered them. *What the devil am I going to do? Need to tell Madge what's happened. Maybe she can control Lettie.* A toxic ball formed in the middle of his stomach.

Chapter 21

Sylvia sighed when the Boston Whaler showed up. The project gathered steam. It was easy to find a VW engine. The fans proved harder. Delbert went through industrial catalogs, poured over specifications to identify the best candidates, then narrowed them down to two. What concerned him was the strength of the fan blades. Would they hold up under flight conditions? Certainly a bird strike would be too much but he could handle that by screening the inlet. He finally decided on one model and ordered two of them, minus their electric motors.

Max stripped the fittings and woodwork out of the Whaler, then built a fiberglass bulkhead down the center of the boat to stiffen the support for the honeycomb panels.

"We can either fill the hull with Styrofoam or you'll have to leave the drain hole in. Water is bound to get in sometime and have to be drained."

"Let's fill it with foam, Max. Then the problem goes away."

It took five panels to cover the hull. Max bonded the first two on the stern end, then shot liquid Styrofoam in and watched it expand to fill the space. The process was repeated for the next two panels. With the last panel at the front of the boat, he shot the foam in and held the panel down until it set. Then he bonded the panel to the hull and trimmed all the way around. They were amazed at how light the finished hull remained.

"How are we going to weld that aluminum frame together, Delbert?"

"I know a guy who can—if I can talk him into it."

"Looks like my next job is to make those two wing spars. We'll have to lay them on the floor corner to corner. There's just enough space."

"Are you starting on that tomorrow morning?"

"I'll lay it out while you are off professoring but I won't cut metal until you check it."

Delbert wheeled into the house to call Tony at the bicycle shop. It took a minute for Tony to place him.

"Oh yes, how's that exercise machine working out?"

"Works like a charm. I've got a new challenge for you."

Tony laughed. "What is it this time?"

"An airplane frame."

"What?"

"A couple of us are building an airplane I've designed. We need some help welding the aluminum frame."

"A real airplane—that flies?"

"It better fly, with the money and work we're putting into it."

"I should say no but you've got me curious. How can I take a look at what you're up to?"

"How about dropping by when you have a free moment?"

"That would be Sunday or Monday, when the store's closed."

They settled on Sunday afternoon. Delbert gave him the address.

* * *

On Friday afternoon, Delbert checked Max's spar layout. It was no surprise to find it precisely right. Max's careful, methodical approach proved ideal for airplane work. The plane wouldn't drop out of the sky because of anything he built.

Cynthia poked her head into the shop on Saturday, curious about the project. She watched Max drilling holes in one of the spars. He had bolted the angle bar to the inboard section. The holes he now drilled passed through both so resin would connect the outside fiberglass layers. Soon she was holding the metal steady for him.

Delbert smiled as he drew plans for the aluminum frame which would tie the hull to the wings and provide support for fans and engine. Originally, he thought the frame must extend to the tail. Max convinced him three bars plus a fiberglass structure would be lighter and stronger.

When Tony showed up on Sunday, the plans were ready.

"You really are building an airplane," he exclaimed.

Cynthia interjected, "If it doesn't fly, we'll turn it into a houseboat."

They laughed. "A little faith, Thia, please." *Truth is, I'm frightened that it won't.*

"Let me look at your plans for the frame," Tony continued.

After a few minutes' study, "Is that all there is?"

"Yes. Well, perhaps not. I may want to talk to you about the joystick linkage when I figure out a design for it. And the drive chain for the fans. The rest of the structure is fiberglass. To be sure the wings and hull are positioned correctly, dimensions must be exact."

"If not, I suppose it will fly around in circles." They all laughed. "Tell you what, if you guys cut the aluminum to the length you want, I'll come and weld it together."

"Fine. Can you give me a cost estimate?"

"It'll cost you a ride in the airplane—but not until it's flown half a dozen times."

"Great. What do you think, Max, can we have them ready by next Friday?"

Max nodded. Tony asked if there was a drawing of the finished airplane. After one look at it he shook his head and said maybe he would wait for a dozen flights. Max and Cynthia went back to drilling holes in the spars.

With the structural design well underway, Delbert turned his attention to flight controls. He had a simple triple channel fly-by-wire system in mind. No control cables required. But he needed six triplex hydraulic actuators sized for light airplane loads. They were a fraction of those on the Avro Arrow and the hydraulic pressure would be one fortieth.

For some time, he felt the mechanical engineering department at UBC might consider it a worthwhile project for fourth year students. The electrical components needed to sense control forces and transmit appropriate signals to the actuators would present a similar challenge to the electrical engineers. Time to call his old friend, Professor Mike Medane.

"Okay Delbert, what are you up to now?"

"What kind of question is that?"

"You only call me when you have a new invention you want to build."

Delbert laughed, "You got me. I have a design project to propose for your students and the mechanical engineering crowd."

"I'm listening."

"Well, don't laugh. I'm building an airplane."

"Mach two or four?"

"This one will do a hundred and fifty knots at best. It's a flying boat."

"Designed so you can fly it, I suppose?"

"Yes. It will be fly-by-wire. That's where I need help. I'm hoping the ME students will take on the challenge of design and fabrication of a triple channel actuator, and your students will design and build the sensor/signal package."

"Sounds simple compared to that digital computer we built for you. Seriously, I'm very interested in it and I think the ME department will be too. Do you have the design requirements worked up?"

"Partially. I can have them in the mail within a week."

"Okay, I'll talk to the involved professors and wait for the data."

"Thanks. Knew I could count on your help."

"You're responsible for the highlights of my academic career. This looks like another episode in the same vein."

Chapter 22

"Have you added up what this project will cost?" Sylvia asked as she served dessert.

"I can't predict it exactly since we are scrounging parts all over the place. So far, we've spent a little over five thousand and the big purchases are done. Mainly what's left is the cost of material like fiberglass, resin, et cetera. Why?"

"Well, we will have Thia's college costs starting after next year."

"Between my pension and salary at the college, we're earning a lot more than we're spending. And there's savings still sitting in the bank."

"Do you still like to teach?"

"I enjoy interaction with students. My method seems to be successful. It would be a sad surprise if they don't keep me on next year."

"I know you're like a kid in a candy store with this airplane project. It just bothers me that it might not get off the water. Also, if it does."

"What did you say, Thia, if it doesn't fly?"

"We can turn it into a houseboat. It will blow its way around the lake."

Sylvia laughed, "You two are irrepressible. If I can't fight you, I better join you. Can I help with the construction?"

"Sure. Max will show you what to do."

"Dad, will you show me how you designed the airplane?"

"Sure Thia. Come into my office in the evening anytime you want—assuming you don't have homework due."

"Thanks, Dad."

He loved the way she called him Dad and got the impression it reflected her appreciation for the solid support they provided. It was almost as if she relied on it as proof that they were still here for her. He understood how there could be a nagging fear in the back of her mind that they might go the way of others that abandoned her. He and Sylvia did their best to keep it buried.

* * *

When Delbert arrived home after Monday classes, he found Max and Sylvia busy fiber-glassing the first side of the two spars. The garage door was open to vent off fumes. Max had blocked up the spars to make sure they were perfectly straight.

"Sylvia and I are making great progress, Delbert. When this side hardens, we'll flip them over and should have them done tomorrow. Two of the web molds are ready so Sylvia can start making webs next."

"You still want to do this, dear?"

"It's fun. I love doing something constructive."

"Beats looking after an invalid, eh?"

"You're as far from an invalid as anything on two wheels."

"Very funny. Have you had lunch?"

"We'll stop as soon as we finish this spar. If you wait, I'll fix sandwiches for both of you."

"Why don't I get started on them. Least I can do is feed the working troops." He wheeled off toward the kitchen.

* * *

After lunch, Sylvia started on the second spar while Max and Delbert laid out and cut aluminum frame pieces. There was a limited amount Delbert could contribute from his wheelchair. He could hold the tape to measure lengths and hold the channels while Max sawed them. It allowed him to feel marginally useful. When it was time to quit for the day, they were pleased with their progress.

Tuesday morning it took all three to flip the spars over. Once realigned, Max showed Sylvia how to make sure the resin penetrated through the drilled holes to bond the sides together. Then he and Delbert turned their attention to the web molds. They were designed with holes to slip over the spars, with flanges top and bottom for bonding skin panels and holes for wires and tubes to run next to the spars. Separate molds were needed for left and right wings so the deflection slots would direct heated air toward the leading edge as it travelled to the wing tips.

Max laid one up as an example for Sylvia. Delbert went back to the actuator requirements. He was confident one design could work in all six locations. By late afternoon, they were ready to mail. Max had one of the two remaining web molds almost done. And the wing spars were finished except for some trimming after the resin hardened.

All three surveyed their work with a feeling of satisfaction. The project looked more feasible than ever. Yet Delbert had a nagging concern about whether the fans could deliver enough thrust to get the plane airborne. He didn't share it with the others.

* * *

Cynthia seemed quieter than usual at dinner. After a while, Sylvia asked what bothered her. Cynthia stared down at the table as though afraid to face them. She hesitated.

"…When I was in withdrawal, I needed something firm to grasp onto and you two were so caring and supportive, you gave me the strength to continue. In my mind you became the parents I never really had. It was so important to me I began to call you Mum and Dad. I sort of adopted you without permission."

Delbert interrupted, "Thia, the happiness you gave me the first time you called me Dad was second only to the happiness Sylvia has given me. My only regret is that we didn't have the joy of watching you grow up."

"That goes for me too, dear."

Tears formed in Cynthia's eyes. Her speech was choked with emotion.

"Thank you…but you are less than ten years older than me. Perhaps I make you feel older than your age—steal part of your youth."

"No, no. I can't speak for Delbert but at times I feel like a mother and at others like an older sister. It's a combination I treasure."

"Me too—well not exactly an older sister." It brought a smile through her tears. "Helping you grow into a fantastic woman is more rewarding than I can put into words."

Cynthia reached out to grasp their hands. All three felt the emotional bond it signified.

"These are tears of happiness…and relief. I'm so lucky!"

"We're all so lucky!"

After a few moments, Sylvia stood up and started to collect dishes to help them move on.

"I better get these washed."

"I'd like to dry for you, but I can't reach the cupboards to put them away."

"Pretty lame excuse Dad. Lucky for you I want to dry."

"Go work on your pet project, dear."

After Delbert left and the dishes were half washed, Cynthia broached another topic tentatively.

"Mum, a boy asked me for a date yesterday. I put him off because I don't know how you feel about me going out."

Sylvia sensed she wanted ground rules even though they had little authority to impose them. It was another facet of the parent role which she had not anticipated.

"You catch me by surprise, Thia. Obviously, we want you to steer clear of exposure to drugs…and alcohol. And it shouldn't compromise your schoolwork. Other than that you should enjoy the teenage experience."

"Except for school functions, how about limiting dates to Friday or Saturday with an eleven o'clock curfew?"

"That seems reasonable. You seem to be a good judge of character so I assume you will be picky about whom you date?"

"Yes…you didn't mention sex?"

"What's your feeling on that?"

"Don't know. I'm confused. Obviously, I'm not a virgin. I try to wipe those memories out of my mind and the idea of sex repulses me. Sometimes it seems like a normal sexual relationship is impossible."

She was close to tears again, not happy ones. Sylvia stopped washing dishes and paused for a minute to gather her thoughts.

"I felt that way after the rape. In fact, for days I felt dirty. Took baths. Nothing helped. It was even worse when periods were missed and I realized part of him was growing inside me. Against the most serious bans of my religion, I had to destroy it. Afterward, there was no desire to ever have sex again. It repulsed me like apparently it does with you now."

"Do you think that can change?"

"I know it can. When the right man comes along, the desire will return. Normally I would never tell you this but strange as it may seem, Delbert and I enjoy a good sex life."

Cynthia smiled, slightly embarrassed by the confession.

"Thanks. You have an uncanny ability to read minds, sense feelings and say the right thing to make problems go away. No wonder everyone loves you."

Sylvia turned back to the dishes. Both women knew the talk brought them to a new level of shared confidences.

Chapter 23

Hank came down with a severe dose of flu the first week of February. Vomiting and a high temperature laid him low. He had to get to Sydney to set up the next drop but when he tried to walk, he slumped exhausted at the door. Madge dragged him back to bed.

"You're not going anywhere today."

He cursed under his breath. If he didn't make the connection the dealers would think his operation had been busted. They might give him one day of grace but after that would sever all ties. Worse still, they may send a hit man to silence him. With no alternative, he told Madge to get Jake.

"You look like death warmed over."

"Get me a scrap of paper and a pencil."

He took out a very small notebook, thumbed through it and wrote down a phone number. He rifled further and wrote down three more numbers.

"You have to run into Sydney and make four phone calls. This one first. Tell them you're Orca and you want to talk to Beluga. Got it?"

"Yeah, Orca to Beluga."

"He will tell you the date and time for the next drop. When you have that, call the other three numbers and ask for the walrus. Each time he will ask who's calling. Tell him Orca and then give him the drop night. The first number is Victoria, the second Vancouver, third U.S. so you need enough coins for the payphone. Four bucks in quarters."

"Okay. I can handle it."

"Call Beluga as close to one this afternoon as you can."

"I've got you covered Hank. Rest and get well before the run."

Madge and Jake exchanged glances on his way out. Both knew the significance of what just happened. It opened the door to continued operation without Hank. He might change the passwords on his next call, that could be a problem. Jake figured it would be too much to hope that Hank wrote the passwords in his little black book.

* * *

"You no sound like Orca," the oriental Beluga said.

"I'm Orca's partner. Orca came down with the flu and is running a high temperature. I've worked with him on missions for over a year now."

There was a long silence. *He hasn't hung up so he must be weighing the risk.*

"You know how dangerous to be imposter? It like death wish."

"That's why I'm telling you the truth."

"Next Tuesday. Ten in evening. Usual place." He hung up.

Jake exhaled. *It worked!* He made the other three calls with a sense of confidence that precluded doubt on their part. His success pumped up his confidence on the trip home. He could run this operation without Jake. Except for the passwords.

* * *

By Tuesday morning, Hank was able to walk around. He was weak, still had a temperature and couldn't keep food down. He insisted he would make the run.

"You sure? I could do it alone."

"No, it takes two people if we're stopped. One to steer and the other to slip the load overboard."

"Madge could go with me."

"I'll go."

Hank was so tired when they set off, he told Jake to drive and slept on the way to the rendezvous. Jake stayed awake to watch for the freighter. When it showed up, he woke Hank and they started out. The pickup went without a hitch. Jake drove them home while Hank kept an eye out for trouble and made sure Jake stayed in safe water.

Back in the boathouse, Jake cleaned things up, stored the unused sugar and hoisted a twenty-kilo package on each shoulder.

"Thanks. Good job tonight."

"Okay, get a good night's sleep."

Hank was still out of sorts the next day. Jake sub-divided the heroin into the three delivery packages. He offered to make the runs alone. Hank wouldn't hear of it. He would never let Jake get his hands on the money first.

Fortunately, the deliveries were made without incident. Perhaps the cold February weather made patrol less popular. Still, Hank was beat when they were done.

On Friday morning, Hank dragged himself out of bed to take Lettie to school and then head off to the bank in Ganges. As soon as Jake saw him head that way, he crossed to the big house. Madge answered the door stark naked. He closed the door and kissed her.

"C'mon, slowpoke." She headed for the bedroom. He was right behind.

They were kissing in the afterglow when Hank came in the front door.

He called, "Madge, I forgot my passbook."

Jake still struggled with his pants when Hank came into the bedroom.

"You son of a bitch! Humping my wife when my back's turned!"

Jake deflected a swing and dodged around him for the door. Hank ran after him, picking up an axe leaning beside the door. Jake was over halfway to the cottage when he tripped and sprawled in the dirt. Hank raised the axe as he approached.

"I'll kill you, you double-crossing bastard."

Jake rolled to one side. Hank turned with him. The axe started down. A shot rang out. Hank arched his back, a shocked look on his face. Jake slid sideways. The axe fell in the dirt beside him. Hank staggered forward two steps and fell face down in the dirt. Madge stood in the doorway, naked, a shotgun in her hands.

"Is he dead?"

Holes shredded Hank's back from the neck down. Many spouted blood. He was either dead or dying. Jake felt for a pulse. There was none. He nodded to Madge.

"Come back to bed."

Later, Jake said, "We've got to do something with him. What will we tell Lettie?"

"I'll handle that. She probably won't be upset. She hates him."

"We can't just bury him like Curt. Sooner or later there will be questions."

"I'll think of something. Pull him out of sight for now. I'll pick up Lettie."

They dressed. Before dragging him behind a shed, Jake searched through Hank's pockets. He found sixteen thousand in Canadian currency and more important, the little black book. *Sixteen thousand, the bastard must have been stiffing me.* He threw an old canvas over the body. Madge was backing the racer out of the boathouse.

Chapter 24

"Where's Dad?"

Jake sat in the kitchen when they entered.

Madge said, "Sit down Lettie. He had an accident."

"Is he dead?"

"I'm afraid so."

"Good."

They were both shocked.

"He was nothing but a mean, selfish man. Did you kill him?"

"Lettie! You're better off not hearing details."

"You did. I know you did. Now Jake can move in with us."

"Lettie!"

"Never mind, Madge. She already guessed that we have a thing going on."

"What will you do with him?" Lettie pursued.

"We don't know yet."

"Why don't you weigh him down with rocks and dump him out in the straits. Then, set the little boat adrift, make it look like he fell overboard fishing and report him missing."

The two adults looked at each other, then stared at Lettie. It was a good plan, a very good plan.

After dinner, Jake cut a section off an old fishnet in the shed. He stripped off Hank's clothes and rolled him onto the net. Then placed a number of boulders beside the body, rolled it up in the net and tied it with rope. It took all three of them to carry him down to the racer. Lettie laughed when she saw the naked body. The bloody back made the cause of death obvious.

"What's so funny?"

"I was just thinking about a dogfish sinking its teeth into his nuts."

Both adults squirmed. Jake threw a canvas over the body in the bottom of the boat. Lettie insisted on going with them and driving. They headed north and out toward the middle of the strait. As they passed the upper end of Gabriola Island, a patrol boat appeared on an intersection course and flagged them to stop.

Jake blurted out, "Holy Christ, what should we do? Make a run for it?"

Lettie responded, "Relax. Don't say anything."

When it came along side, Lettie showed a generous portion of leg, gave them a big smile and shouted.

"Am I doing something wrong, Officer?"

All eyes on the boat were on her. "You were too fast for this channel, young lady."

"I'm sorry. I didn't know. Please don't arrest me."

"I'm not going to arrest you. Just make sure you slow down through here in future." A number of sailors wished he would arrest her.

Jake nodded. His throat too constricted to talk. Madge trembled. The patrol boat pulled away down the channel. Lettie laughed as she started off again.

"That was close."

"Too close," Jake agreed. Madge shook violently now that the danger passed.

It was dark when they reached a good drop point. They turned off the running lights for the last five minutes. Now they drifted slowly as Jake and Madge struggled to lift Hank's body over the side. It splashed, then slowly sank out of sight. Bubbles surfaced for a few minutes. Then all was calm. Lettie started back for home under Jake's guidance. He stayed well out in the middle of the channels.

Back home, they washed out the boat. An hour later, they loaded fishing equipment in the small boat. Madge took it up the channel. Jake followed in the racer. At a location which made sense from a fishing viewpoint, she dropped a rod and gaff hook to float off, climbed into the racer and set the little boat adrift.

"That should make it look like he fell in trying to land a fish."

"If they're ever found."

Early Saturday morning Jake and Madge drove the racer to Cowichan Bay and called the police. Madge did her best imitation of panic.

"My husband went fishing yesterday evening and he hasn't returned. We tried to find him last night. Help us, please."

"What is his name and where would he be fishing?"

"Hank Morgan. He usually fishes near Swartz Bay."

"We'll get a search started, Ma'am. What's your name and how can we reach you?"

"Madge Morgan. We live at Musgrave's Landing. We don't have a phone."

"What kind of a boat was he in?"

"It's a white boat with an Evinrude motor."

"How big?"

"I don't know…about sixteen feet…or do you mean the motor? I think it's fifteen horsepower."

"Okay Ma'am. Best you go home and leave it to us. We'll find him and send someone to notify you when we do. Or this afternoon regardless."

"Thank you."

She turned to Jake after hanging up, "Did I sound convincing?"

"Good job. We better hustle home and make sure there's no evidence left around."

It took an hour to go over the boathouse, yard and shed area. Jake took Hank's clothes and boots up the trail and hid them in the cave. He would bury them later. Madge cooked breakfast for the three of them before it dawned that Jake should be fixing and eating his own breakfast in the cottage. He carried his food over, slid it onto one of his plates and returned Madge's dish.

He decided to fry some more bacon and an egg, made his own coffee and ate. It would be safer to leave the dirty dishes in the sink. He stopped suddenly, then bolted to the door.

He burst into the main house, "What clothes would Hank take fishing?"

"Damn it, yes. We need to get rid of them."

She rummaged around and returned with a red plaid jacket and a pair of gum boots.

"Other than this he would be wearing what he had on."

Jake carried them up to the cave. He had misgivings about leaving the things there. *What if they bring dogs? I better take these further up and bury them in the woods.* He returned for a shovel and one of the waterproof canvases they used for deliveries. *The dogs won't be able to follow the scent with his stuff sealed inside.*

As an extra precaution, he walked a quarter of a mile up a small creek, then into a dense wooded area and dug a hole two feet deep. He piled rocks over the package and covered them with dirt, then scattered brush over the spot and took a different route home.

Chapter 25

Late in the afternoon, a patrol boat entered the bay. It towed their boat behind. Madge and Lettie both screamed when it came in view. They raced down to the dock.

"Did you find him? Where is he?"

Cal Lockhart stepped onto the dock followed by his wife, Mattie. The two Salt Spring Island police officers stopped in front of Madge.

"Madge Morgan?"

"Yes."

Cal continued, "Madge, as you can see we found the boat. That is your boat, isn't it?"

"Yes."

"There was no sign of your husband with the boat. We found a fishing rod and a gaff hook not far from the boat but that's all."

Mattie spoke up, "Did Hank wear a hat when he fished?"

Madge trembled, "Sometimes. Did you find one?"

"No, which is surprising. Usually when someone falls in the water, things like hats come off and float away."

"As far as I can remember he wasn't wearing one yesterday."

"The other curious thing—there wasn't much line played out."

"Played out?"

"Yes, if he was landing a salmon and fell in, one would expect some line to be played out from the reel."

Mattie walked past Madge and Lettie to where Jake stood.

"Hi, I'm Officer Lockhart." She held out her hand.

Jake shook hands. "Jake Moran."

"Moran...Morgan without the 'g'. Any relation to Hank?"

"No. Hank hired me to help work the farm."

Mattie looked around. "How big a farm is it?"

"Mainly just over two hundred sheep, a cow, three pigs and a bunch of chickens. Grow our own vegetables too. We run the sheep on the hills mostly."

"Does the girl go to school?"

"Lettie goes to school over in Cowichan Bay. We run her back and forth each day."

"We?"

"Usually Madge or Hank but quite often me."

Mattie moved closer and asked quietly, "Any reason Hank would want to take off? Marital problems? Cabin fever?"

"Not that I can think of. He seemed happy enough with his wife and daughter. He liked the isolation here. More than me, for sure."

"You don't get into town often enough?"

"It gets pretty lonely here for a single guy."

"Still you stay?"

"The pay's okay. Don't know what will happen with Hank gone."

"We don't know he's gone yet."

"Well, yes, you know what I mean, if he is dead."

"Where do you live?"

Jake didn't like all the questions. They made him nervous.

"In that cottage. The Morgan's live in the main house."

"I assumed that." She strolled toward the shed, looked around and came back to where Cal stood with Madge.

"I was just telling Madge that we will continue the search tomorrow through Monday. If he did drown—and I'm not suggesting he did—his body would come to the surface by then so we would know for sure."

"Thank you," Madge mumbled. Mattie had surreptitiously studied Lettie off and on during their time on the landing. Other than the initial scream, she had shown little sign of emotion or distress. She seemed content to merely watch.

Cal continued, "Will you be alright here alone for the next while?"

Madge glanced at Jake. "Yes, we're fine. Jake can keep the farm running." Jake nodded.

"We'll get back to you when we have more news."

The two officers boarded the patrol boat and shoved off. The crewman had tied the small boat to the dock and lifted the motor out of the water. The fishing rod and gaff hook was inside.

* * *

Mattie sat next to Cal in the boat.

"Something's fishy, if you'll pardon the expression," she said.

"What do you mean?"

"No line played out. Nothing else floating."

"You're always suspicious, honey."

"Why wasn't there a weight on the line? A lure by itself will just ride on the surface."

Cal paused. "That's an interesting point."

"Jake talked like Hank was already dead. And the girl. She was not one bit upset that her father is missing. For that matter, Madge is not all that grief-stricken either."

"So you don't think he drowned?"

"I think he either took off or was murdered."

"Well, let's give it a few days to see if a body shows up."

"Good old Cal, always wanting to give everything a few days to play out." She laughed and jabbed him in the ribs.

* * *

That female cop is suspicious," Jake commented.

Madge countered, "Cops are paid to be suspicious. There's no evidence for her to go on."

"I don't like it. We need to be careful until it blows over."

"She looks like a real live Wonder Woman," Lettie tossed out.

They turned to her. "Don't let her looks fool you. She could spell trouble."

"Well, she's not going to sneak up and spy on us."

"All I'm saying, Madge, is we need to keep playing the role until they call the search off."

Lettie laughed, "You'll be lonely in the cottage all by yourself, Jake." He scowled. *Your time will come.*

* * *

For the next two days, Jake and Madge joined in the search to show they worried. On Monday, they dropped Lettie off at school and pretended to search until noon. Then they headed to Sydney to refuel and fill their Jerry Cans. Jake had a phone call to make. When Beluga came on the line, he recognized Jake's voice.

"Orca still sick?"

"It died."

After a pause, "What now?"

"We can continue as before."

"Nothing change?"

"Nothing."

"How die?"

"Drowned. No trace left."

"You same place."

"Yes."

"Okay new Orca. Week from Wednesday. Half past ten in evening."

"Perfect."

"Better be."

* * *

"We need to make a run next week. Think you and I can handle it?"

"Sure Jake, as long as those cops have gone back into their shells."

Jake made the other three phone calls to set up the deliveries. Then they headed back to the search. Just before picking Lettie up they ran into the patrol boat. Cal told them there was no sign of Hank. They decided to call off the search but would list him as a missing person in case police spotted him somewhere else.

Jake and Madge felt a sense of relief as they collected Lettie and headed home. Madge cooked a celebration dinner. They broke out a bottle of wine.

Lettie scowled when Jake followed Madge into the bedroom. She waited until she could hear them making love, then undressed and crept into the room. Jake was the first to feel the second naked body.

"Lettie, what are you doing here?"

"I want some of the action too."

She hugged them both. Her hands ran over their bodies as she kissed the back of his neck.

"No Lettie, this is wrong…Madge?"

It seemed unreal to him that Madge remained calm, seemed to take it in stride.

"It's been a lonely life here for all of us, Jake."

"But she's your daughter."

Lettie whispered in his ear, "Relax Jake, we both want to fuck you and it's more fun together."

"Let her stay. I don't mind sharing. You're man enough for both of us."

It wasn't the way he dreamed of making out with Lettie. More exciting by far. The two women seemed to work together in a way that thrilled him beyond his wildest dreams. It seemed immoral, at least certainly unnatural for mother and daughter to be in the same bed but he didn't dwell on it for long.

Chapter 26

By the third week of February, there was an assortment of aluminum bars, channels and brackets mounted on the hull. A stack of wing webs sat in the corner. Max and Sylvia were laying up skin panels on two molds that Max produced for inboard and outboard sections of the wing.

Delbert had finished the flight control design. At first he planned to use a joystick on the left side only. When Cynthia saw that she complained.

"How can you teach me to fly when there's no way to do it from the other side?"

"Who said I'm going to teach you to fly?"

"Why not? Besides, what if something happens to you or your controls in flight? There should be backup."

Delbert smiled, "You're right."

Dual joystick design proved difficult. When one moved the other had to track it. He went through a number of possibilities before settling on a relatively simple linkage. It actually allowed a more robust sensor arrangement. He thanked Cynthia for pushing him into the dual system and promised to give her lessons.

The linkage was an ideal task for Tony. After review of the design, he indicated there could be as much as two hundred dollars in parts.

Now Delbert had the data needed to give Mike Medane design requirements for the sensor package. He would mail them off after a phone call.

"Delbert, the mechanical engineering students are having a ball designing your actuators. Professor Smith asked if you have anything else to add."

"They could build me a dual tank hydraulic reservoir."

"Whatever that is. Send me a drawing."

"In a few weeks I could have a real challenge for them. A water jet assembly. It would be a joint project with your students."

"Fantastic. You better get it to us soon. We're into the second term now."

That adjusted Delbert's priorities. He wanted the water jet to extend down behind the whaler's transom and be steerable. It would take water in from the front up through an outer cylinder, pass it through the pump to be sent back down in an inner pipe directed out the back. It had to telescope to retract in flight and it had to rotate through a full circle. As a design project, it would separate out the best students.

The water jet allowed the plane to be handled like a boat for docking, unlike most seaplanes which are steered toward the moorage with the power cut in time to let them drift to a stop. They require the pilot or someone to jump out and hold the plane until mooring lines are tied. Delbert wanted full control during docking. The water jet would let him propel the plane forward, backward, turn and stop.

Sylvia and Max were still making wing panels when the fans showed up. On the weekend Tony appeared. His interest in the project piqued, he wanted to help with more of the construction. Under Delbert's direction, he shock-mounted the fans. Now Max could see how the inlet ducts should be shaped. Sylvia and Cynthia carried on with wing panels while he started to cut and shape pressed paperboard sheets.

The compound curves meant the ducts would need to be made in pieces and patched together. At one point, Delbert thought it an impossible task. He admired Max's patience and perseverance. If one approach failed, he simply stepped back and tried another. Gradually the inlet shells emerged.

"Max, you're a genius."

"When you're happy with it, I'll reinforce it on the outside to make it rigid."

"Great. Then we need to wrap it with insulation for sound-proofing and add an outer casing."

"What if we make the outer casing with a gap and fill it with Styrofoam?"

"Let me check on the sound deadening quality of Styrofoam first and get back to you."

Delbert spent the evening sketching his concept for the water jet. He included dimensions and design requirements. The package was ready to mail next morning. After classes, he wheeled to the college library and researched the sound characteristics of Styrofoam. Max's approach looked feasible.

As Sylvia cleaned up to cook dinner, she talked to Delbert over her shoulder.

"You know, Max does a lot of work on your project."

"It's our project now. You're doing almost as much as him."

"Don't you think we should pay him something?"

"You mean to cover his expenses, travel, tools and things like that?"

"As a minimum. Something more would be a good gesture of our appreciation."

"Doubt if he would take much more but I'll see what I can come up with."

* * *

Toward the end of the first Friday morning class, Delbert decided to address a nagging concern.

"We have over a month together now. Do you like my approach, or would you prefer to return to conventional lectures?"

He received what seemed like unanimous support.

"Fine. In that case, let's talk a little about human nature. I think of it as a person's automatic response to situations confronted. Some result in good things. For example, in a crisis some people accomplish extraordinary feats with what seems like total disregard for the risk involved.

"On the other side of the coin, human behavior can lead well-meaning individuals to take the easy road, ride on other people's coat-tails. Now I know most of you are like Charlie, dedicated, hard-working…"

Laughter interrupted him. Everyone knew Charlie was the class party boy. Even he laughed.

"…but I'm worried that there may be some of you who let things slide until assigned a task for class. Our approach is on trial here. We need you all to demonstrate on exams that it works. So here's what I want you to do. Write down page 164, questions one, two, four, seven and eight.

"Answer them on a sheet of paper and turn it in to me next Friday. Work on your own. If Charlie or anyone asks you for help, refuse. You will not be graded on this test. I just want to get a progress check. A professor I worked with at UBC says there's nothing worse than marking test papers and he only marks them because it's demanded. I side with him. I won't mark your papers next week. I'll just scan them to uncover weaknesses."

He repeated the assignment for the second class.

* * *

Over the weekend, Tony made pipe extensions to connect to each fan shaft and run forward through the inlet duct into the engine compartment. He slid a bearing on to later be bonded to the inlet and plug the gap. On the forward end he mounted sprocket wheels. He would use a motorcycle chain to connect them to the engine driveshaft. Delbert picked wheel sizes which would drive the fans at design speed with an engine running at thirty-five hundred revolutions per minute.

Construction progress led Delbert to think they might have an airplane by summer. *Don't get too optimistic*, he cautioned himself, *there's a million details to work out. Roadblocks are bound to crop up.* The question of whether the fans could deliver enough thrust still bothered him.

* * *

Delbert scanned the submitted papers Friday afternoon. Results were good, not perfect, perhaps a little better than expected even though he had set his sights high. He fed back comments Monday morning. To begin, he held up a sheet of paper titled "Assignment" with the numbers one, two, four, seven and eight spaced down the left side. The rest of the sheet was blank.

"This is Charlie's effort."

Everyone laughed. Charlie smirked.

"You didn't fool me Charlie. I knew there would be a second sheet with your name on it. Good job by the way."

Charlie smiled. The prank maintained his class reputation yet revealed his mastery of the material.

"All in all, as a class you did well. There are a couple of you I will get in touch with for a little extra mentoring. Mid-terms are a month away. I intend to give a small weekly assignment until then." *Will it be enough?*

Chapter 27

"Madge, work on the farm is too much for me on top of the runs. We need help."

"Where can we find someone trustworthy who will keep their nose out of our operation?"

"One guy who comes to mind is Luke Adams. He does our shearing. He knows sheep. Only downside is he turns nasty when he's boozed up."

"Would he stay out here?"

"Daresay, if the money's right. He may even work into the operation. There was a rumor he pedals drugs to a few islanders. We can afford to pay him a good salary."

"Well, feel him out. Incidentally, Hank had a lot of money in the Ganges bank, and I think one in Port Angeles. Problem is I can't get access to either one."

"Why not?"

"The accounts are in his name."

"Don't you inherit them?"

"Perhaps eventually but as far as I know he had no will and he isn't even declared dead."

"Why don't you write a will for him?"

"That's a thought."

Madge gathered papers with Hank's handwriting. After careful study, she put tracing paper over a few good examples and traced what he wrote. Then she rewrote the passages and compared them with the original. There were differences. She practiced over and over until the match seemed passable.

It took much more practice to duplicate his signature. To be authentic it had to be written quickly as he would have done. After five days she decided to try a will. The first step was to compose it in Hank's typical wording. Then she wrote it out and compared the result with Hank's papers. Jake studied it as well. They agreed it looked good.

Madge wrote it out again on a fresh piece of paper:

I, Henry Samuel Morgan, if I should die, do hereby give all my worldly goods to my wife, Magdalene Mary Morgan. If she be dead before me, I then give them to my daughter, Henrietta Amanda Morgan.

Signed this 6th day of July, 1958.

Henry S. Morgan

They studied the final draft in detail. It matched Hank's writing and signature perfectly to their untrained eyes. Madge wrote "Hank Morgan's Will" on an envelope, folded the will to fit and placed both outside to lie in the sun and weather. It would take a few days to get all sides aged.

* * *

The bank manager in Ganges read the will.

"This is highly unusual. He should have had it notarized by an attorney and officially recorded."

"Hank was never much for formality. I need access to the bank account to keep the farm afloat. What can I do?" She added a little tremor to her voice.

"Well, we would have to let a judge pass on this. Where's the death certificate?"

"I don't have one. Hank drowned three weeks ago but they never found his body."

"That makes it even more difficult. You should have the police declare him missing and presumed dead."

"I'll do that. Then, will you help me with the judge thing?"

"Yes."

Madge took back the will and walked to the police station. Cal appeared when she rang his bell. *That's lucky. His wife would make this a lot harder.*

"Captain, my husband never saw fit to use a joint bank account. Now our money is tied up and I need access to some of it to run the farm. Need to pay Jake and shearing comes soon. The bank manager says I need a statement from you which declares him missing and presumed dead."

"Well, it's now three weeks since he disappeared. Surprised that his body didn't surface. To be brutally frank, it leads me to think he took off and is alive somewhere."

"Are you telling me I have to wait forever for a man who is either dead or probably never returning? I can't survive without some of our savings."

Cal could see the woman's distress. He figured if Hank was still alive, he would have run out of cash by now and tried to withdraw more.

"Let me call the bank manager and talk it over. Sit down and relax."

He left the room and called the bank.

"James, got the Morgan woman here. Before I give her a missing, presumed dead statement, can you tell me if Hank Morgan has tried to make a withdrawal or written any cheques in the past three weeks?"

"I can check on that for you."

He was off the line for five minutes.

"Captain, just between you and me, there's been nothing so far. The only thing that allows me to reveal that is you're conducting a police investigation, understand?"

"Sure, James. Loose Lips, if you're listening you didn't hear anything, or you can kiss your job goodbye."

A female voice replied, "Mum's the word, Captain."

Cal shook his head and returned to the office.

"Okay, Madge. I'll write out the statement for you."

"Thank you, thank you so much."

Back at the bank, she gave both papers to the manager.

"Mrs. Morgan, the circuit judge stops here on Monday. I'll present these to him and get a ruling. Normally, this would go to a probate court but perhaps he will grant you access to the account on a hardship basis. Can you come back Tuesday?"

"Yes Sir. I'm very grateful for your help."

* * *

Jake waited for her at the boat.

"How did it go?"

"Okay, I think. The cop gave me a death statement and the bank manager will run it by a judge on Monday."

"I got hold of Luke Adams. He's cool to the idea but he's willing to come and look it over."

"We can pick him up on Tuesday."

"Let me call him back and see if he can meet us then at one."

Chapter 28

Madge stared at the brand-new passbook. The single entry of current balance astounded her. Unable to suppress a smile, she thanked the manager.

"This is such a relief."

"Here's a cheque book. Keep your account number in a safe place. You need to enter it on the cheques."

"Can I withdraw some funds now?"

"Certainly, how much?"

"I need a month's supplies and I had to borrow two hundred from Jake Moran. Seven hundred dollars should be plenty."

She couldn't contain her excitement when she met up with Jake.

"Got it. Here's the two hundred you lent me. We're rich, Jake. Can't imagine how much is in the U.S. bank."

"Great, kid. Let's do the shopping before Luke shows up."

An hour in Mouat's store required three trips to haul supplies to the boat. Then they walked over to the White Elephant Café and enjoyed a leisurely lunch. Luke appeared just after one. His eye wandered over Madge's body in appreciation when they were introduced. Her ego flattered, she invited him to sit down and join them in a cup of coffee.

"Jake tells me you have over two hundred head of sheep for me to shear."

"Yes, and lambs to take care of. We sell them through a wholesaler in Victoria. The sheep pretty much take care of themselves the rest of the year."

"You're talking about a part-time job?"

"No, full-time. There's other work on the farm. We grow a lot of vegetables and berries. There's three dozen fruit trees."

"You got a tractor?"

"An old Fordson. It's time we bought a new one. You could help us with that."

"What does it pay?"

"I can guarantee you a minimum of three hundred a week."

Jake looked at her. Luke raised his eyebrows.

He stood up, "Let's go see the place."

* * *

On the ride home, Luke liked the way the wind lifted her dress from time to time. *This job could prove real interesting and the money's good.* Jake realized he needed to straighten Luke out on one thing, Madge was his.

"Great boat you got here."

Jake responded, "Yeah, it's a racer. Keeps us from wasting time running back and forth."

It could have more uses than that, Luke thought. Jake decided Lettie would be out of school by now. He dropped in to Cowichan Bay to wait for her. She arrived five minutes later. Madge did the introductions.

"Luke, this is my daughter Lettie. Lettie, Luke Adams. Luke may come to work the farm."

"That's nice."

She gave him a seductive smile. Handsome and with a good physique, he immediately attracted her. The appeal was mutual. *This gets better every minute. Better remain aloof or she might cut back the offer.* He fought the urge to ogle the two women on the trip across the narrows.

The two men carried the heavy supplies up to the house. The women handled the lighter stuff. It took only two trips.

"Jake, why don't you show Luke the farm while I fix dinner."

When the men left, Lettie exclaimed, "He's as handsome as Jake. Do you think he'll take the job?"

"Hard to tell. I hope so. We need another man around here."

"I agree with that!"

"To run the farm and our operation, you shameless hussy."

"Does he know about the operation?"

"No. He's bound to figure it out soon."

"Can he be trusted?"

"My intuition tells me he's a scoundrel and therefore will fit in well."

* * *

"Jake, there's a lot of work here for parts of the year but it's hard to see enough income from the farm to pay us the likes of three hundred a week."

"She can afford it."

"She's never stiffed you?" he laughed, "salary I mean."

Jake chuckled, "No, the money's good. Just so you know, she's my woman now so don't get any ideas about her."

"Looks like there's enough of them to go around."

"Tread lightly, Luke."

"I hear you. Let me be frank. There's more going on here than farming. And I'm game for whatever it is. So you know you can trust me, I do a little drug pedaling to three wealthy islanders every two weeks. Pick the stuff up in Victoria. I want to continue that."

"The last thing we need is to have drug trafficking tied into our operation."

"Operation?"

"Farm. How much does that net you?"

"Sixty bucks every two weeks."

"That's penny ante stuff which we can't afford have hang over our heads. If you want this job, tell your Victoria contact to send someone else out every other week."

They must be running drugs here. It's a perfect setup. That means big money if—when they let me in on the operation. They neared the main house again.

"Where would I bunk down?"

"In that cottage. I used to cook my own meals there but it makes sense to at least eat dinner together, if Madge agrees."

"Well, she's got herself a hired hand."

Chapter 29

Dean Farquhar intercepted Delbert in the main corridor.

"How do you like the lecture world now that you have nearly two months under your belt?"

"Fine. I enjoy the challenge." *Does he know I've strayed from the traditional lecture format?* "I should confess that I use more give and take with the students than the typical lecture formula."

"As a matter of fact, I've heard rumors about that."

"I do progress checks on the students regularly. They appear to master the material and their participation in class is outstanding. Other than sickness, attendance is one hundred percent."

"No need to go on the defense. Must admit it causes me concern, but I harken back to what Dean Calder said. We'll get a feel for your method's success during mid-terms in March."

"Thank you, Dean. We won't betray your confidence."

As they parted, Delbert realized he had tensed. Afraid the dean would order him back to the traditional approach. He knew that would leave him frustrated and probably make the job unpalatable. Now at least he had until mid-terms to show success. Would the students come through for him?

* * *

Dan Martin called that evening. Delbert lived with the Head of the Electrical Engineering department and his wife Samantha while at UBC. They were like second parents. Dan taught Delbert to fly.

"Mike tells me you're building an airplane."

I should have told him sooner. "Yes. It started with an attempt to design a flying boat that is both quiet and can be controlled by hands only. It's kind of snowballed."

"Quiet?"

"My goal is to patrol the local waters and ferret out drug smuggling runs for the police. That requires an airplane that can't be heard."

"Sounds like quite a challenge. Where are you at with it?"

"The design is firm except for a multitude of small details. Chuck Lansbury's father is helping build it. He's an expert on fiberglass construction. Sylvia, Cynthia and a custom bicycle maker help as well."

Dan laughed. "Not a lot of aircraft experience there. I'd love to see this thing. Mind if I fly over on Saturday? You can bring me up to speed on your paying job as well."

"That would be great! Why not stay overnight?"

"Don't want to impose—or slow down construction."

"Don't worry about either. We have a big house now with extra bedrooms. Would Samantha come too?"

"Could ask her. Actually, it would make more sense to bring Jack. His aircraft mechanic background might provide some useful advice."

"Bring them both."

"Okay, I'll pursue that and let you know."

Half an hour later, Dan called back.

"They both can come. Are you sure it won't be too much for Sylvia?"

"Mentioned it to her. She looks forward to seeing you two again and Jack is no problem. Says she'll pick you up at the airport if you give us a time."

"Feel like we're putting you out."

"No way."

"Well, I'll schedule us to arrive at eleven in the morning."

"You mean eleven hundred hours." They hung up with a laugh.

* * *

The two men were anxious to see the shop, so Samantha and Sylvia carried in bags and started to fix lunch for everyone. Cynthia was laying up a skin panel while Max and Delbert aligned the spars in a support jig Max conjured up. Delbert introduced everyone.

Dan and Jack stared at framework, fans and duct pieces mounted on the hull, somewhat dumbfounded.

Jack opened with, "This is going to be an airplane?"

"Guess it looks a little strange at the moment. Let me run through the design with you."

They moved to where Delbert had drawings piled on a card table. He reviewed concepts first, then covered more novel design features.

Dan asked, "Will you get enough thrust out of those fans?"

"That's a burning question. My calculations say yes. And I think because they are ducted, we can drive them beyond their rated speed without cavitation."

Delbert fielded a number of other questions. Jack was more interested in controls, electronics and hydraulics. When they ran out of things to ask, Jack brought up an intriguing possibility.

"You know Delbert, a student ground looped a Cessna one fifty a couple of months ago. Totaled it. Insurance company paid up and gave it to me to scrap. Not enough in it for them to bother with. There's a lot of things you could use directly."

"The whole business of electronics and instruments is something I've put off. To find a cheap source for things like that will be a hassle."

"Not if I strip them out of the one fifty. Could pull out all the panels, wiring, lights, everything. Most of it you could use as is."

"Can you do that? Be phenomenal. You'd have to give me a cost figure."

"That's easy. No cost. That stuff brings almost nothing as scrap. Consider it my contribution to the drug war."

"That would be a wonderful windfall."

"It'll take a couple of weeks to strip it. Then I'll load it in my pickup and haul it over. Maybe help you with some of the installation too, if you want."

"You know, this thing started as a pipe dream which I doubted would ever materialize. But people like Max, Tony and now you are rapidly turning it into a reality."

Cynthia spoke up. "You could give Mum a little credit also, Dad."

"Right, Thia, and you too."

Dan smiled at her use of the Mum and Dad. They're a family of three. She's a lucky girl. On the other hand, they seem to be lucky parents as well. What a long way Delbert has come from the unsure boy who showed up at our doorstep six years ago. He's lived more in these years than most do in a lifetime. It's amazing how he rises to each new challenge or catastrophe and turns it into another victory.

Chapter 30

Max declined an invitation to stay for dinner. The airplane continued to dominate conversation while they ate. Both Dan and Jack expressed curiosity about how the flight controls would work. It pleased Dan to hear of the UBC student involvement. He recalled how beneficial Delbert's scanner projects had turned out. This seemed to follow in their footsteps. Nothing fired student enthusiasm more than a real-world project.

"You realize you will need to give all those student contributors a ride when it's done."

"That would be my pleasure."

"Are you confident they can produce a fail-safe package of actuators?"

"You bet. They have to develop a rigorous test program as part of the project. No different than if they were in industry."

"Maybe I'll tell Mike to let them know I will review the test results."

Jack chimed in, "You know, hydraulic pumps could be pricey."

"That's a concern even though we only need a hundred psi."

"I seem to recall the Bonanza has an electric hydraulic pump. If not, I'm pretty sure some of the bigger amphibians do. I'll scrounge around and see if I can locate something."

"We need at least one electric one, preferably two. One mechanical one could be driven off the engine if necessary. Be wonderful if you can find some."

Samantha pulled the conversation into a new direction by asking Delbert about his professor job. He gave them a run-down on his technique and admitted his concern that the students do well on the mid-term exams. The progress checks showed promise yet he would remain on edge until the results were in.

"I'm not sure I could return to formal lectures now," he confessed.

Dan agreed. "Even though I've given a good many of them over the years, I can't say they were a joy. Nothing beats class participation."

Sylvia asked about their son Charlie and his wife Virginia. Samantha responded.

"They're in Calgary now, as you know. Their little boy is growing fast. He's a delightful little devil, always smiling, hardly ever cries. Sleeps through the night already. I think Virginia's pregnant again. She doesn't admit it but she has that telltale glow."

"It scared me when they said they intended to name him after me. No boy should be saddled with a name like Delbert."

"Delbert Martin might sound a bit awkward but it's Del Martin and that fits him well."

"Does he have a middle name?"

"That is his middle name. He's Daniel Del Martin."

"Oh, Daniel of the Martin," Delbert laughed. "At least he can change to Dan if he wants."

"Oh no. They insist he will always be called Del."

Sylvia smiled. It was just like Delbert to belittle his influence on others. She knew how strong all the Martins felt toward him in both friendship and respect.

Samantha steered the conversation to Cynthia. Asked her what grade she was in and what extracurricular activities she was involved with.

"I'm in grade eleven. I'm on the girls' volleyball team and the swim team. I'm also on the Student Annual committee."

"You're very active. What about after high school?

Flustered, Cynthia looked at her parents. They had not discussed college. She couldn't speak for them.

"I don't know," she stammered slightly.

Delbert intervened. "We hope she goes on to college. Suppose you haven't given much thought to that yet, have you Thia?"

Cynthia brightened. "I used to think I would like to be a doctor and guess I still do, although lately aerodynamics has captured my interest too."

Jack said, "You better keep the doctor avenue open in case that contraption in the shop never makes it off the water."

They all laughed. Cynthia replied with confidence, "It will fly."

Delbert added, "Why do people often refer to my designs as contraptions?"

"Because they are always so new and different from what people expect, dear."

Dan added, "And far more ambitious than most people think achievable."

* * *

On Sunday nearly a full crew worked in the shop. Sylvia and Samantha went shopping. Dan helped Max and Tony mount webs on the wing spars. They had to be located precisely, then bonded to the spars by Max while Dan and Tony held them in position. Delbert and Cynthia continued to lay up the rest of the upper skin panels. Jack poured over the plans to find equipment locations and determine wire and tube routes. Then he moved to the airplane skeleton and wing assembly to measure the length of hydraulic tubing and wire required.

Samantha interrupted them at one o'clock.

"Lunch is served on the deck."

Over pie and tea Dan said, "That was fun. Wish we could stay on but I'm afraid we better head back this afternoon."

Max said, "The extra hands sure helped in setting those webs. We can start mounting the upper skins now with confidence."

"You know, Delbert," Jack injected, "when I first looked at that rig in the shop, it looked absurd. I wondered how anyone would find a way to let you down easy. But the more I studied it, the better it looked. You really do have an airplane there."

"Thanks, with your background, that means a lot."

The women hugged. Men shook hands. Then Sylvia drove the three visitors back to the airport.

Chapter 31

Luke's first week on the farm brought him up to speed in a hurry. Sheep required almost no attention though that would change later in the Spring. Madge and Lettie looked after the chickens and fed the pigs. The cow was another story. Luke had to milk her morning and night. Not his favorite job and he could see it would compromise his effort to join in the other activities he knew took place.

He wanted to be included in the drug business. Although obviously lucrative, there was a second reason to gain their confidence. The women. In just a week, the loneliness of nights in the cottage began to wear on him. He envied Jake and wanted a piece of the action. *He's got Madge to keep him warm. I want Lettie. She teases me with that come and get it look. Madge would fire me if she caught us together.*

They had fallen into a routine. Luke joined the other three for dinner in the main house. After coffee and some conversation, he would return to the cottage. Sometimes it took a hint to prompt him to leave. The cottage was cold and lonely in the evening.

On Wednesday, Madge told him dinner would be an hour early. From the cottage, he watched Jake and her leave in the boat at six-thirty. *Maybe I should go see what Lettie's up to. No, better not—don't know how long they'll be gone. Damn, this is getting old fast.* He read some more of a decrepit book he found in the cottage. Then, frustrated, snuffed out the lamp and went to bed.

Within minutes, he heard the door open and close. He could see Lettie in the moonlight that found its way through the window.

"Want some company?" she asked in a sultry voice.

"You know I do but what if Madge comes back?"

"They won't be home before midnight."

She was a vision as she undressed in the dim light. Both were naked when she slipped into bed. It wasn't the first time he felt a mild concern about the age of a sex partner. It wouldn't be the last either. He lived for the thrill of seducing an innocent teenager but soon realized this one was not innocent. She left him an hour and a half later.

Luke slept soundly when the boat returned. He didn't hear Jake pass by with two packages on his shoulders nor Madge close the boathouse door with a bang. She was still annoyed when Jake returned.

"We never would have found the second package where you wanted to search."

"Okay Madge, give me a break. I misread the tide. That's all."

"Things like that could put us out of business. I'm sure we're on probation with them now until we build a success record."

"It won't happen again."

"Sorry Jake, I shouldn't chip at you. Let's go to bed. I'm beat."

Jake was too. It didn't bother him that she wanted to skip sex. He was surprised that Lettie was asleep in her own bed. Her appetite seemed insatiable.

While Luke was milking the cow next morning, Jake retrieved one of the packages to subdivide it for the local runs. The two smaller packages he kept hidden in the house during the day. It bothered the couple to have that exposure. At dusk, they set off with the Victoria package. Luke watched them go, then crossed to the main house. Lettie answered his knock.

"How about a repeat performance?"

"Not now. They'll be back in less than an hour. When they make the second run I'll come over." She kissed him and pushed him away.

Luke was lying on his bed when he heard them return. He got up to spy on them. After a few minutes in the house they headed back to the boat. Jake carried a package on his shoulder. *Got to be heroin to make a package that size worth smuggling. They picked it up last night and are delivering it tonight.* The boat was barely out of the bay when Lettie slipped into the cottage.

She was back in bed with him again the next night. He liked the drug business even if he had no part of it. Life took a great turn for the better. He wondered how often the drugs were dropped for them. All of a sudden it couldn't be often enough.

* * *

"What's the deal with Lettie? She's slept alone the last three nights."

"What's the matter Jake? Don't I keep you busy enough?"

"It's not that. Frankly the two of you wear me out—in a damn good way. Just surprised at the change. Is it a bad time of the month?"

"No, our periods are at the same time. I think she's found a new playmate."

"Luke?"

"Probably."

The thought that she would dump him for Luke bothered his ego. *Why let it bug me? Two of them are more than I can handle anyway.* Madge read his thoughts.

"What's the matter? Is the old bull mad about losing part of his herd?"

Jake laughed. "You're more than enough woman for me. I'm just wondering how involved we want to get Luke."

"Between the salary and Lettie, he's not going to leave for a long time."

"Doesn't her sex life bother you?"

"It's her business as long as she doesn't get pregnant. I've drummed the importance of protecting against that into her head."

"Well, you're right about Luke. He won't leave now."

"Let's make sure you won't either."

Later, as Jake stared up at the ceiling, "Madge, we can't go on hiding the operation from Luke. He knows it exists. Why don't we take the plunge and cut him in?"

She thought about it. *I would like to stay out of the boat during drug runs. If they're caught, I can claim I thought they were out fishing. Lettie can keep Luke under control.*

"Okay, but the two of you still have to maintain the farm and offer him only twenty-five percent of the take."

"I'll talk to him in the morning."

"I'll tell Lettie she can move in with him."

He felt a momentary pang of regret…and concern.

Chapter 32

Two weeks after their visit, Jack showed up with a pickup load of airplane parts. The wing panels were finished. Work was progressing on the flaps. Tony built the linkages, shaft and bearings. Delbert and Sylvia laid up sections in Max's molds. Max was well on his way to finishing the inner skin of the inlets. He planned to add ridges on the outside to hold the outer skin and stiffen the structure before pulling it off the paper mold.

After sorting and storing pieces, Jack installed wiring in the wing for navigation lights and hydraulic tubing to the mid-wing fence. Two tubes ran right behind the front spar and two more in front of the rear spar. Wires to carry the aileron and flap actuator signals followed the same route.

When Delbert agreed the installation was complete, Max bonded the wires and tubes to each web they passed through. They then flipped the wing over and bonded on the lower wing skin panels. Completion of the wing structure felt like a milestone even though flaps and ailerons remained to add. The wing would be mounted onto the body in the shop to make sure everything fit and was in alignment. Then they would disconnect it again for transport to Elk Lake.

The airplane is coming together faster than I could have imagined. The more we put into it, the more I worry about it flying. There's too much speculation regarding what thrust those fans will generate. I'll look like a fool if it just flounders across the water. What if it just tips on its tail and sinks? Have some confidence. You know that won't happen. If it lifts off the water, it will fly. That's the hardest part. He made sure the others didn't see his concern, especially Sylvia.

In fact, the airplane was not his only concern. His students wrote their mid-term exams this week. He had created quite a difficult test, fair but comprehensive. Would they perform to his expectations? More important, to the dean's expectations? He was almost afraid to start marking papers. No point in procrastinating, he spent the evening grading a batch.

The first dozen showed a good trend. Eighty percent or higher with a number near perfect. His elation increased with each new paper. In the end, there was no failing grade in either of the two classes. He turned in the marks with a sense of pride in what they accomplished. On Monday he greeted each class with the news.

"In a word, you did well. Guess that's three words. Let me add two more, thank you. Seriously, not one person failed and in general, the grades were high. I'm proud of you. Give yourself a hand." He clapped. They joined in, laughing.

The dean caught him after his second class.

"Delbert, I looked at the grades you turned in. They were abnormally high."

"The students did a fine job."

"Perhaps. Or was the test too easy?"

"I tried to make it difficult but fair and comprehensive."

"May I have a copy of the test?"

"Certainly." *He thinks I fed them a simple test.*

"I trust you didn't tip off the test questions ahead of time?"

"Before the test? It wouldn't be a test if I did that." *Doesn't he trust me?*

"Well, either your approach works really well or they found the test too easy. I sincerely hope it's the former. I'll look this over to gain confidence. We'll have to find a way to give them more difficulty on finals so there will be a better spread of marks."

"I understand, although if a student masters a subject, it seems he or she should be rewarded accordingly."

"Can't argue against that. I'll get back to you if I see a problem with this. In the meantime, press on."

Delbert gathered his things and headed home. The euphoria of congratulating students for a job well done gave way to turbulent thoughts.

I worried for weeks whether my system would succeed or not. Then the day the proof arrives, the dean doesn't believe it. Is he just looking for a way to force me back to lectures? He seems like a reasonable man. Is it one more example of human aversion to change? Can I dig my heels in if he insists on going back? My imaginary heels? Claim the proof is in the results? What option do I have if he insists the test was too easy? Damn it Delbert, don't worry about it until he forces the issue.

Sylvia noticed he came home distraught after leaving in such high spirits earlier.

"What's the matter?"

"My students did so well on the exam, the dean thinks the questions must have been too easy. Or worse, that I tipped them off."

"Were they or did you?"

"No."

"Then he'll have a hard time making his case."

"Unless I'm guilty until proven innocent."

"Would it make any sense to give the students last year's test, perhaps without giving them a chance to prepare? Or would that be too risky?"

Delbert thought for a minute. "That makes a lot of sense! You're a genius, honey."

"There's only one genius in this family. I want to talk to you about something else."

"What?"

"I had my appointment with Doctor Simpson this morning."

"That's right. What did he say?"

"He did a thorough examination. He says one fallopian tube was essentially destroyed but the other is intact. It can and probably does deliver eggs. But he doesn't know if they can attach to the uterus if fertilized because of the scar tissue. If I become pregnant, the chance of a miscarriage is high. Yet he thinks I could possibly carry a baby and deliver it through a caesarian. There's a lot of if's involved."

"But there is a chance. How do you feel about that?"

"We both need to think it over. Perhaps because of my Catholic upbringing, I lean toward letting God decide if and when I become pregnant."

"If you do get pregnant, I want some of the credit too."

She gave him a good-natured push which sent him rolling backwards. He let the chair roll while he laughed until it hit the wall.

"Delbert!" A tone of good-natured reproach in her voice.

"Seriously, honey, I'm fine with that approach. You know me. My view is more physical than theological. I believe your body will decide the issue both on pregnancy and miscarriage."

"Then should we go off the rhythm method?"

"I'm in favor of that."

* * *

Delbert found himself humming as he worked on the airplane. Soon Max was humming the same tune. That fact dawned on them when Sylvia joined in too. They broke out laughing. Delbert broke the silence that followed.

"You're doing such a fine job, if this thing doesn't get off the water we can donate it to a museum as an example of outstanding fiberglass construction."

"It will fly, although it wouldn't bother me if it didn't."

"Are you still worried I'll get shot down by smugglers?"

"Don't make light of it, they're evil people."

"I hear you."

Max interceded. "Maybe we can get Chuck to fly cover for you."

"He would get dizzy zipping back and forth trying to stay near me chugging along at a hundred knots." They chuckled at the thought.

"On a serious note, we need to figure out what to do about the windshield. I can't mold the front end until we have one."

"Sylvia, when you reach a break point, how about driving me to a junkyard?"

Delbert measured the width of the hull and jotted down junkyard addresses from the phone book. They set off. It took two stops to find one the right size with no tinting and a compatible electric windshield wiper system. When Max saw the windshield wiper he shook his head.

"That won't work over seventy knots. It'll just lift off the glass."

"Not if we add a little airflow deflector that forces it against the windshield at higher speeds."

"Maybe."

Max is right to be skeptical. There are so many things we're guessing at.

* * *

Tuesday morning Delbert made a special trip in to talk with the dean. He suggested they pull out the previous year's mid-term exam and give half to each class without warning. They could scratch any topics not in this year's curriculum. Delbert didn't think any needed to be removed.

"Delbert, I'm weak on Physics, however, the test appeared substantial."

"I would like to remove any doubt about its validity."

"Okay, it'll provide an interesting data point."

The dean had an assistant go through the files and retrieve last year's exam. Together, they went through it and decided to simply alternate the questions between the two classes. The resulting tests were typed up and administered on Friday.

Delbert spent the weekend marking papers. The more he marked, the more he smiled. These tests were simpler than the one he created, and the students came through admirably. He delivered the results to the dean on Monday.

"Okay, Delbert, you've proved your case. Maybe I should have some of the other professors monitor your classes," he said with a laugh.

Chapter 33

Luke poured the morning's milk into the milk can, pushed the lid on and carried it to the creek. The cool mountain stream kept the milk from souring for a couple of days at least. As he washed out the milk pail, Jake called him to join them in the house. *What's this all about? Do they know about Lettie? Are they going to fire me?*

Jake and Madge were waiting for him. "Sit down Luke."

"I do something wrong?"

"No. We figure you have a pretty good idea the farm is a sideline here." Luke remained silent.

"No need to play dumb. We've decided to offer you a chance to participate. If you're not interested, you can go on with the farming as you have been."

Jake paused. Luke's heart skipped a beat. *I'm worried about the job and they're offering something twice as good.*

"I don't know exactly what you're up to but I am sure enough interested in participating."

While Madge watched him, Jake described their operation. The more Luke heard, the more excited he became. It took an effort to stay calm.

"You and I will make the runs. Your cut will be twenty-five percent. In addition to your base pay, for weeks where there is a run you stand to make an extra three thousand Canadian and four thousand American. Madge will milk the cow when we are away. You still do it the rest of the time and between us we run the farm. Interested?"

"Sure am."

"You need to commit all the way. We're working for some mean people. Any screw-up, crossing them or blabbing and they won't hesitate to send hit men to silence us all. That's why you had to give up that little supply service and it's why you can't go off drinking in town—ever."

"How do you enjoy all the money you're making?"

"We'll shut down the operation in a year or two. All good things come to an end sooner or later. And we can probably work out some time off in Vancouver when things are quiet, providing we can trust you to stay off the booze."

Madge and Jake exchanged glances. Then she said, "Lettie will move in with you."

Luke stared at her, speechless. Does she know? Does she really mean it? Maybe she's fishing. He said nothing.

Madge laughed. "Relax, Luke. I'm sure she's tested the water already and will jump at the opportunity. She will certainly take away one incentive for trips to Vancouver."

"You got me buffaloed. Don't know what to say."

"How about thanks?"

Jake and Madge rehashed the conversation after Luke left.

"He's a greedy bastard just like us. I think it will work out."

"He practically wet his pants when you told him about Lettie."

"One thing for sure, if there's any problem, there will have to be a hunting accident."

* * *

Luke returned to his cottage alone after dinner. He had a hard time keeping his hungry eyes off Lettie while they ate. Madge chuckled to herself. She hadn't had a chance to talk to Lettie. Luke began to doubt Madge's sincerity earlier. *Was she just pulling my leg? Good thing I played dumb.*

When Madge described the new situation to Lettie, she cautioned her.

"We're counting on you to keep him entertained and if he says or does anything to make you think he's no longer loyal to us, promise you will tell us right away."

"I will."

"And make sure you don't get pregnant! That would ruin everything. Does a man good to go without sex for a while. They appreciate it more afterward."

"I know."

Lettie practically skipped across to the cottage and into Luke's arms. He couldn't believe his good fortune. Jake and Madge shared concern over the new arrangement. They would have to keep an eye peeled for trouble.

Luke joined Jake for the runs on the following week. He was a quick learner when it came to driving the racer and his eyesight was even better than Jake's. He spotted both buoys first. Jake showed him how to rig the sugar anchor and how to slip it over the side discreetly. Also, how to spot patrol boats.

He reported back to Madge that it looked like they would make a good team.

"That's funny. Lettie says the same thing. He better get busy with the shearing between runs. It's a big job. You need to take care of his other chores and help out."

"You sound like Hank giving orders."

She grabbed his shirt. "Don't ever say that again!"

"I was just kidding."

"Don't! Don't ever compare me with him."

"Okay," he wanted to change the subject, "did you find the U.S. bank passbook?"

"No. I've searched everywhere in the house, even the boathouse and racer. I can't find it anywhere."

"What about the attic or under the house?"

"I would have spotted him going under the house but take a look if you want. The access panel to the attic is in his office. Check that out too. It takes a ladder to get up there and he would have a hard time hauling that in and out without me seeing him."

"Perhaps there's a pull-down ladder or rope ladder."

"Take a look."

Jake started under the house with a flashlight. The mass of cobwebs he ran into convinced him no one had been there for years. Still, he searched around and found nothing.

He carried a short ladder in and used it to push up the attic access panel. More cobwebs to push through and no sign of a pull-down ladder. Between cobwebs and dust, it was obvious

Hank had not used the attic. Frustrated, he sat down in the office. Madge came in.

"Nothing?"

"Nothing. It must be somewhere. What did he do before a run to the bank?"

"Nothing special. He spent some time in here with the door closed. Didn't want to be disturbed when doing his accounts."

"Accounts? I don't see any account books."

Jake scanned the room. Madge had been through his makeshift desk and everything else. He carried the ladder outside and decided to make another pass through the room. An hour later he still had no clue where the passbook might be hidden. *Where could it be? Where would I hide it? Some place the women couldn't get at it. In a wall. Under the floor.*

He worked his way around the four walls, searching for a panel, pressing and tapping all over them. They were solid. He noticed the door had a latch on the inside which showed signs of wear. *He must have locked it to keep them out.* Next, he went over the desk inch by inch. No secret compartment. That left the floor. It looked solid as well.

He crawled around, inspecting boards close up and pushing down on them. It seemed fruitless until he pressed a short board near the wall beside the desk and felt upward pressure on his knee. He stood up and reached over with his foot to press down on the board again. As the wall end went down it pushed up a section of adjacent boards. Jake got his fingers under them and lifted.

The panel consisted of boards of different lengths to camouflage its purpose. Under it was a box suspended between the floor joists, a box with bundles of American money. *He didn't have a U.S. bank account! He kept it all here! Should I tell Madge. I could keep on the same way. No, don't even think of double-crossing her. Besides it's more fun to live off it together anyway.*

"Madge!" he shouted.

She came running. "Oh, my God!"

He stood up. She threw her arms around him. They kissed.

"We're rich! Let's count it."

It came to six hundred and five thousand dollars. They couldn't stop laughing. After putting it all back, they closed the lid and decided to celebrate in bed.

There was enough money to give up the operation any time they wanted. It would be easy to live in style somewhere in Central or South America. The American dollars would be greedily accepted with no questions asked. When they discussed this, Madge said they would have to make a quick, clean break to avoid being shot by the kingpin. That would be a problem with Lettie. They better keep on for now.

Chapter 34

Through March and early April momentum increased on the airplane. It was an illusion because big pieces were built and added to the framework. With the nose section in place and the wings mounted on the body, it almost looked like an airplane. What remained was fiddly stuff, mostly inside. Progress was no longer apparent to the casual observer.

Tony and Jack were both caught up in the project. Tony spent the best part of Sundays and Mondays working with Max to install controls and moveable surfaces. He fabricated the metal parts and together they mounted them on the structure. Jack showed up each Friday night and worked Saturday through mid-afternoon on Sunday installing panels, wire and electronics.

"My wife suspects I'm having an affair over here, Delbert."

"An affair with the project perhaps. Why not bring her over for a shopping holiday in Victoria next weekend?"

"Don't want to impose on you and Sylvia."

Sylvia broke in, "Don't be silly. Bring her over."

Professor Smith carried the actuator assemblies over in person. He wanted to see how they would be used. The quality produced by the students was impressive. Delbert snickered when he saw a small "UBC" stamped on casings, followed by the year. He showed the professor where they went and promised to send photographs after they were installed. The hydraulic reservoirs were handed over also.

"The jet pump is a tremendous challenge for them—the kind of project they could spend a whole year on. With telescoping and three hundred sixty-degree rotation, it's an intricate design which requires precise machining. All the pieces are built. They will assemble it next week. Mike Medane has given us the drive motor and sensor package. We'll test in the water tank within two weeks."

"Wonderful!"

"Some of the students have put long hours in on these projects. I stress that they keep up with their other work, but you can't hold them back."

"Well, it gives them a picture of the real world that awaits them."

"By the way, we tested these actuators with a hundred psi hydraulic pressure. Slammed them back and forth. They have clever snubbers in each end so you can't damage them."

The professor took some pictures of the planned actuator locations and headed back to Vancouver. Tony and Max were excited about installing the actuators so they could check out their rigidity and surface travel. They needed a hydraulic pump to truly check them out.

Tony, Jack and Delbert talked it over. The cheapest pump set up would be to drive the primary channel from the engine and use an electric pump for the secondary channel. Jack agreed to search for the pumps and accumulators next week. Tuesday night he phoned.

"Delbert, there's a war surplus store downtown that has three small hydraulic pumps and accumulators that were pulled out of a Canso amphibian. They look serviceable. They want a hundred and eighty for each pump and accumulator package."

"Can you buy two of them? I'll pay you this weekend."

"Sure. They also have a small emergency hand pump for thirty-five if you're interested."

"You know it would be good to have that backup since we would have no control if both powered pumps fail."

"I'll bring them over on the weekend."

* * *

To an untrained eye, the airplane looked almost complete. It still lacked side doors and windows but inside the seats, panels and controls were all in place. Seats on the right side, that is. The floor on the left side had two hold-down clamps. Delbert had rolled up a makeshift ramp, turned and moved forward to his desired position. They positioned the clamps there. He was excited to play with the joysticks, imagining what it would feel like in the air.

Mike Medane called with news that the sensor packages were ready.

"Can we send two of our top students over to mount and check them out? Dean Calder says the university will pay their lodging."

"They can stay with us. How long will they be here?"

"I'd say up to three days."

"How would it be if they come over on the Marguerite on Monday afternoon? We'll pick them up."

That worked. Mike gave Delbert names and descriptions. When Delbert told Sylvia they were coming, he couldn't help adding a comment.

"Honey, we're almost running a bed and breakfast these days."

"With everything except payment."

"Do you want me to cease and desist?"

"No, no. It's exciting to see it all come together and our guests are good company."

* * *

The two students, Tom and Bill, were better than good company. Their enthusiasm was contagious. Delbert spent Tuesday morning with them explaining where sensors were to be mounted and showing them the wire runs to be used. When he arrived home Wednesday afternoon, they had everything connected and ready to test.

Bill worked the hand pump to build up hydraulic pressure. Tom gently moved the joystick to the left and they watched the ailerons deflect. It worked!

Soon they were moving the joystick in all directions and cheering when the controls behaved as they should. Next they tried the small joystick mounted on the aisle stand. Its forward motion controlled engine speed. Sideways motion controlled the rudder which is what they wanted to check. It too worked. Finally, they moved the flap lever to its takeoff position. The flaps deflected down along with the ailerons. Moving the main joystick correctly deflected the ailerons from their new position.

The flaps deflected full down when the lever was put in the landing detent.

"Everything works perfectly," Delbert told them. "Now we need to calibrate it all. Measure surface deflection versus control position and make any adjustments needed."

Chapter 35

On Thursday evening the phone rang. Delbert answered it and was greeted with a gravelly voice.

"Delbert?"

"Bentwing, is that you?"

"How are you, son?"

"Fine. Where are you?"

"Comox. Any chance we could get together tomorrow if I drop by?"

"Love to see you."

"I'll fly down to Pat Bay in the morning and catch a cab to your place."

Delbert gave him the address. Bentwing Carson was head of the RCAF Training Command, Delbert's superior during his flight test days.

* * *

After greetings and pleasantries, Bentwing wanted to know what Delbert did with his time these days. They first discussed the professor assignment. Then Bentwing's ears perked up when Delbert mentioned the seaplane.

"Designing and building your own plane? This I've got to see."

Delbert took him out to the shop. Bentwing's jaw dropped at the sight.

"Hi Sylvia. He's put you to work on this? Damn, you're even more beautiful than I remembered."

"A compliment like that wins you a free lunch. I'll go fix it for us all."

After introducing him to Max, pointing out he was Chuck Lansbury's father, Bentwing allowed that Chuck was his best pilot now that Delbert was out of the business.

"The boy lives to fly jets," Max replied.

Delbert went through his usual spiel about the design.

"I know better than to question you, son, but must admit to a bit of skepticism about its ability to fly. Guess I'm too used to sleek birds."

After lunch, Bentwing confessed that his doctor insisted he walk two miles a day.

"He tried to ground me because my ticker isn't what it used to be. Told him there was always an experienced pilot with me who could land the plane if I conked out. Took a bit of brow-beating but he finally relented."

"Want to get your two miles in now?"

"Can you wheel that far or do I have to push you?"

Delbert laughed. "I roll an eight-kilometer circuit four times a week. Come on."

They set off down the street, a short, bandy-legged man beside a wheelchair inhabitant. Sylvia knew the two friends wanted to talk over old times. She smiled as she watched them go.

After glancing around to be sure no one was close, Bentwing asked, "You ever think of that Arrow sitting in its bunker?"

"Often. I can picture that beauty as if I was standing in front of it. Sometimes I even dream I'm flying it."

Bentwing sighed. "It was surely a beauty, alright."

"Is a beauty."

"No sign of it anymore. There's a hundred-foot band of mowed grass along the side of the runway. Beyond that a wheat field."

"Will it ever be unearthed?"

"Not in my lifetime. Maybe in yours. Who knows? By that time, you'll be the only one who knows where it is."

"What a tragedy?"

Bentwing looked down at the wheelchair. "Life is full of tragedies."

* * *

A major milestone occurred on April thirtieth. They opened the garage doors and started the engine for the first time. The airplane, with wings attached, was angled to fit in the shop. With the engine idling, there was an almost imperceptible whoosh of air from the fans. Without gages, it would be hard to tell the engine was running.

Max had the airplane tethered to the garage with ropes. The moment Delbert both anticipated and dreaded arrived. He slowly advanced power. The fans accelerated and airflow built up. Tension on the ropes increased and Delbert felt the familiar strain to leap forward against parking brakes. He gave the others a radiant thumb's up.

Cynthia walked closer to the exhaust and was nearly blown over. She pulled back laughing. They all cheered when Delbert brought the engine back to idle, waited a minute and shut it down.

* * *

The water jet assembly arrived mid-May. Three of them spent a day mounting it on the hull transom. It was an impressive piece of machinery. Sylvia took photographs of it extended and retracted to send back to the students. She included pictures of the installed actuators and joystick controls. Delbert added a letter to congratulate the students.

Max asked what color they should paint the craft.

Tony jumped in. "White with a bright red racing stripe down the side."

"No," Delbert responded, "it has to be a dull matte grey. We want it hard to see as well as hear."

* * *

At the last session of each of his two classes, Delbert left his students with parting advise.

"Do you now see the wisdom of understanding class material rather than blindly copying lecture scribbling's?"

There was a resounding yes.

"I want to suggest a technique for the dry lectures you will encounter. Divide yourselves into packs—two, three, however many you want. For each lecture, assign one person to write notes. Rotate the assignment. The remainder of the pack just watch and jot down important points.

"If any of the pack can find a page in the textbook that covers the material on the board, signal the others and stop copying the notes. Highlight the important points or write them in the margin. If the material is not covered in the book, the scribe should make copies for other members of the pack. The important point is to spend as much time as possible understanding the topic. Discuss the material within your pack on your own time."

At the end of each final class, students broke out in a round of applause. It embarrassed Delbert though he felt a sense of gratitude.

He regretted the time needed to mark final exams. He was eager to test everything on the airplane. At the dean's insistence, the exam was difficult and the spread of marks reflected that. Still, everyone passed.

* * *

By the first week of June, it was time to launch the plane. Max and Tony propped up the wings and disconnected them from the body. Delbert bought a used boat trailer and rented a flat-bed truck. It took all of them to carry out the wing assembly and place it on the truck. It sat there on its sponsons while Max blocked it up to provide additional supports.

With the boat trailer connected to his pickup, Max backed it up to the front of the airplane body. The trailer winch pulled it on. They set off to the public boat ramp at Elk Lake in a caravan.

Delbert's anxiety level rose. *Will it actually lift off the water? Will I be able to fly again?*

Chapter 36

It took five days to round up the flock. Each day all four would head off in a new direction and walk beyond the furthest point they expected to find sheep. Then, they spread out to sweep the stretch back to the farm. Each knot of sheep was herded along. Soon stragglers would join the flock automatically. By the time they reached the farm there would be fifty to a hundred to drive into a small holding area. Once secure, a gate was opened and they were driven into a large adjoining field with the rest of the flock.

They counted two hundred and five sheep and a hundred and forty-one lambs. Luke didn't look forward to that much shearing. He preferred drug runs but realized that was the price he had to pay. In two days, the next run would give him a break. Jake cut out the sheep and brought them to him. Madge carried wool to the barn. Though Luke sheared fast and efficiently, it soon proved hard on his wrist and back.

With two drug run breaks, it took three weeks to cover the flock. In the process, Jake separated out all but fifty female lambs and two healthy males. These fifty-two rejoined the flock and were turned loose for another year. The remaining lambs would be sold.

"How do we get wool and lambs to market?"

"Sven Johansson has an old Navy landing barge over in Sydney. I call the buyer and he arranges with Sven to bring a truck over to pick up the wool. We'll keep the lambs in the pasture for a month to gain weight."

"That how you get a new tractor here too?"

"Thanks for the reminder. I'll get on Madge about that."

While Jake was in Victoria selling wool, he priced a new Ford tractor. On his return, Madge wrote a cheque for it. Two days later Sven showed up with a truck to haul the wool. He ran the barge up until it grounded on the beach, then dropped the front-end ramp. The truck drove off and up to the barn. Sven waited while they loaded wool and tied a tarp down over it. There was enough wool for two truckloads.

With the truck back on the barge, they watched Sven raise the ramp, back off the beach and chug away. Jake went with them after hitching a ride with the driver back into Victoria. He bought the tractor on the basis that the dealer would take back the old Fordson in exchange for arranging and paying for delivery on Sven's barge. He came back with the truck and driver to pick up the second load the next day. A week later the tractor arrived and the exchange completed.

Jake had Sven deliver four drums of gasoline along with the tractor and gave him four empty drums to take back. That would cover both boat and tractor needs for the summer.

* * *

After a drug pick up in early May, Luke asked how he divided the local package.

"I'll show you. Bring one of the packages down to the shed. Before you cross the open area, scan the narrows to be sure there's no boat heading our way."

He was waiting when Luke arrived with the package. Jake broke the seal and opened it.

"It's simple. Each of these packages is one kilo. We just count out five for Victoria. I usually count the rest to be sure there's fifteen of them, but they never make a mistake."

"Pretty simple."

"Sure. Now I wrap the five packages in this plastic and tape it up tight. Then wrap that in a piece of canvas like this and tie it with this light rope. The trick is to make this loop to snap on the buoy."

"If you do the same with the Vancouver batch, how about letting me do it?"

"Be my guest. You can use their canvas over the plastic."

Luke duplicated the first package. Jake tested the loop to be sure it wouldn't pull out. Luke carried the larger package back up to the cave after checking for boats again.

It had been a good Spring for them. Only once did they have to slip a shipment over the side and come back later to retrieve it. They did have to change the drop point on the American side to further out beyond Port Angeles near Crescent Bay. It gave them a shorter run from the shelter at Sooke and allowed them to scan for patrol boats before making a high-speed run across.

* * *

After the next collection run, Luke offered to divvy up the local packages. When he had it open in the shed, he slipped a very small amount of heroin from a number of packages into an envelope. *They won't miss this.* He folded the envelope in his pocket, wrapped the packages and carried the Vancouver one back up the hill. He stashed the envelope in his cottage while Lettie was in school.

Two weeks later he divided the next package. Jake and Madge left to buy supplies in Ganges. He had time to take a pinch from all twenty kilo packages. *Doubt if the dealers weigh these and even if they do, could they detect the shortfall. Hell the suppliers probably make sure they have a little extra anyway.* The stash in the cottage was now significant when one realized it would be cut seven to one with sugar before use.

Chapter 37

Max pulled into a vacant area of the parking lot. The truck stopped nearby. With Max and the truck driver on one sponson and Tony and Jack on the other, they lifted the wings off the flat bed and carried them across. They had to raise them to clear the pickup cab before moving back to mate with the body.

While the other three steadied the wings, Max climbed up on the trailer and described how to jockey them into position. He inserted four bolts on the corners first, then added the intermediate ones. With the wings secure, he hooked up the hydraulic lines and wire bundles.

"Before I fasten on the access panels, let's test for leaks and surface operation. Can we start the engine here?"

"Jack can. Don't run it above idle though."

Jack laughed. "Be funny if I blew it off the trailer."

"Not as funny as you might think," Delbert replied.

Jack climbed up into the cab and started the engine. Then checked each control surface to confirm the connections were correct. After shutting down, Max climbed up and looked for leaks, then fastened on the access panels. They were ready to launch.

"Say the word, Delbert, and we'll dump it in the water."

"I'm almost afraid to…Oh heck, go for it."

Max carefully backed the trailer down the ramp to the water's edge. They untied the hold-down lines before he backed it further. Delbert noticed with relief that it floated reasonably high in the water. *The stern's slightly lower than the bow but pilot weight will balance that out. So far so good.*

Tony snapped a rope on the eye bolt in the bow and gently pulled the plane around to the float next to the ramp. They pulled out bumpers and moored it to the float. Max lowered the ramp door, Delbert wheeled up into the cockpit and locked himself in position. He opened the window to talk.

"After I start the engine, I want to check out the water jet. Give me slack on the rope but don't let go of it."

With the engine idling to keep from running the batteries down, he extended the water jet, turned it to swing the stern out and ramped up the pump. The plane reacted quickly. *I've got to use less power to maneuver. It packs more punch than I thought it would.* He gently backed the plane away from the float then brought it in again and docked it.

"Works great. Unhook the line. I want to take it for a spin."

In minutes, he taxied out into the lake, made a number of turns, backed it up and finally brought it back in to dock at the float on the opposite side. Sylvia took photographs.

"Hop in Max and Tony."

After he took them for a spin, he repeated the process with Jack and Sylvia. Cynthia hopped in before them and crouched behind Delbert. They all agreed it was an exciting boat ride if nothing more. But would it fly?

Delbert dropped off the passengers, then spent half an hour going over everything on the airplane: radios, controls, lights, hydraulics, battery condition and charging. It all checked out. He followed his test pilot training.

"I want to take it out and do some taxi runs."

"Be careful, dear."

"I will."

On the water, he slowly advanced power. The fans spun up and the airplane started forward. By the time he reached the fan design speed, the plane was accelerating nicely. He tested the roll control and rudder. They responded quickly. The airplane was now skipping over the water. He decreased power to check landing stability as it decelerated. He was far down the lake now. Time to turn back. With the engine at idle, the plane still skimmed across the water though it slowed gradually.

That's not like most seaplanes. It hydroplanes on the whaler hull. He moved the water jet to the reverse position and applied power. That brought a safer deceleration. He turned around to head back. This time he wanted to see how fast it would go with just the water jet. It reached about twenty knots. Then he advanced power again with flaps in takeoff position.

When it reached fifty knots, he pulled back the power. It showed no sign of lifting off but then he hadn't rotated the nose up. The float was approaching at an alarming rate. He applied full reverse water jet and watched everyone run for high ground. Once he knew it would stop in time he laughed. They returned as he taxied to the float.

"Did I scare you? Can't tell you how much fun this is! It handles beautifully but it doesn't want to slow once it hydroplanes. Have to use the water jet to decelerate. We'll have to allow for that if the water jet is inoperative."

Jack asked, "Did it lift off?"

"No. I kept the nose down. At the recommended fan speed, it took quite a while to reach fifty knots. I want to make another run to see how far I can advance power without losing the fans."

That alarmed Sylvia. "Losing the fans?"

"I mean until there's cavitation, dear, not until they blow off. If there's no surprise, I'll try lifting off on the return run."

At forty-seven hundred RPM he felt the thrust drop off. Cavitation. The thrust returned when he slowed the engine below forty-five hundred RPM. *Good. We can go a thousand RPM above the fan design speed. It accelerated faster. Is it enough for takeoff? Time to get this machine stopped.* He resorted again to the water jet.

On the return run he ran the engine at four thousand RPM. At sixty knots, he gently raised the nose. It lifted free of the water! Elated, he set the airplane down again and decelerated. At the dock, he maneuvered so that Jack could inspect the fans.

"They look normal to me. No sign of distortion."

"Okay. Time to see how it flies."

He taxied out and applied power. They had their fingers crossed except for Sylvia. She said a prayer for his safety.

At sixty knots, Delbert raised the nose. It lifted off and climbed steadily. He banked into a turn to follow the lake shoreline in case something failed. At a thousand feet he levelled off and reduced power to maintain ninety knots. *It responds perfectly to the controls. I'm flying again! I'm really flying again!*

While one part of him paid attention to the airplane on the lookout for any sign of a problem, another side of his mind savored the flight. *A rat in a drainpipe is confined to one dimension. A cow still earthbound in a field experiences two degrees of freedom. Only soaring birds and darting fish enjoy three degrees of freedom. And so do pilots!*

Though he flew the airplane with care reserved for a newborn infant, he knew in time its capabilities would be enjoyed. Not like the freedom of a supersonic fighter, but a thrill in its own right. He no longer sat in a wheelchair.

His reverie interrupted as he flew over the dock, he waved to the cheering crew. At the far end of the lake, he flew away from the water, turned to a crosswind leg and then set up the approach. He had the lake to himself, no boats in sight. With flaps still in the takeoff position, he felt safe landing at seventy knots. The airplane skipped once then settled onto the water. He let it run out toward the dock.

It dawned on him that the fans might provide drag if he shut down the engine. When he tried it, deceleration increased dramatically. *Okay, that's how to get it stopped when the water jet is unavailable.* He docked without restarting the engine.

Jack noticed the complete silence first. "Is the engine running?"

"I shut it down to see if we could get some drag from the fans to decelerate after landing."

They were all excited. Tony exclaimed, "It really flies!"

Cynthia sounded indignant, "Of course it does."

Max and Sylvia just smiled. She sensed Delbert's elation. *If only he wouldn't use it to create mortal enemies.*

Chapter 38

"When can we go for a ride, Dad?"

"Not until I wring it out. We need to see how it stalls and at what speeds. I have to expand the speed/altitude envelope and simply build up some hours to be sure it's safe."

"You sound like a test pilot," Sylvia pointed out.

"I am one again." His happy grin was infectious.

They decided to park it on the trailer overnight. Tony pulled it over to where Max had backed the trailer down the ramp. They winched it on and tied it down. Max towed it out and backed it to a rear corner of the parking lot.

Jack climbed up and inspected the fans more closely to be sure there was no damage. Moving inside, he started the engine and checked it out along with the electrical and hydraulic systems. It all passed muster under his critical mechanic's eye.

"Max, how about backing your pick-up under the wing so I can stand on it and inspect the flaps and ailerons?"

Max complied. Jack peered in, tried to wiggle the control surfaces, then had Tony climb into the cockpit and move them while he applied some resistance. They repeated the process for the other wing and then the tail.

"Everything looks shipshape," he pronounced.

A number of people collected around the strange aircraft. Delbert answered questions about it while Jack locked the two doors. They reluctantly left it for the night.

* * *

"We need to find a safer place to store it."

"Does it have to be a lake?" Sylvia asked.

"Preferably. It would be less exposed to storm action, especially moored in the water. Elk Lake could work if we can find a private dock to rent. It's a little small and so crowded in the summer though."

"What other lakes are there?"

"Thetis is too small, Shawnigan too far away, Langford would work. Guess we could use the Saanich inlet, the Gorge or Esquimalt. Those three are open to the sea and the airplane could be spotted by a boat cruising around."

"Sounds like Langford Lake is close enough yet pretty secluded." *Face it, he's dead set on patrolling for smugglers.*

"It looks the best alright. Let's drive out Monday afternoon and look for a moorage."

* * *

The owner of a small grocery close by Langford Lake put them onto an old couple who lived on the lake and had a float that he thought they no longer used. Delbert and Sylvia followed his directions down a narrow paved road which led around the southeast end of the lake. Jim and Edith Brown's house was right where described. Jim answered their knock.

"Jim, I was told you might be interested in renting your dock for me to moor my seaplane."

"Don't think we want noisy planes here on the lake."

"Mine is very, very quiet. You won't even hear it taking off."

"Every airplane I ever heard has been noisy."

"How about if I fly it in, taxi here, then takeoff again? If you think it's too noisy, we'll look elsewhere. I believe you will find it's quieter than any motorboats on the lake. The question is, if you agree it's quiet enough, will you consider renting the dock?"

"How many people would be coming and going?"

"Usually just me and perhaps a passenger. It only holds three people."

Jim glanced at the wheelchair. "You fly it yourself?"

"Yes. It's designed to be flown by hands only."

"What do you use it for?"

"Pleasure mainly. It gives me a way to get back in the air after my accident."

Jim's eyes widened. "Say, are you that Pillage fellow who landed a jet on the golf course last year?"

Delbert laughed. "I would hardly call it a landing but yes, that was me."

"People still talk about how you must have saved a lot of lives doing that instead of parachuting to safety."

Delbert said nothing.

"Look, I'd like to help you Mr. Pillage if your airplane is really as quiet as you make out. When would you fly her in?"

"Tomorrow morning."

Delbert had another reason to desire this moorage out of the public eye on a fairly secluded lake. Elk Lake was too busy during warm weather. Before long, this strange machine would draw media attention. He preferred a low profile to avoid advertising the whereabouts of his patrol craft.

Chapter 39

Max helped launch the plane again. There was plenty of fuel for a day of flying so Delbert told them he would be gone for four hours. Sylvia and Max watched him take off.

"You know, Sylvia, this has been a great experience. Feels like we accomplished something extraordinary."

"You made it possible. Flying means so much to Delbert, it sometimes makes me feel like his second love."

"No question in my mind you are his true love. I see the way he looks at you and hear what he says to you."

"Thanks Max. He's always had my love. Now he's rescued his flying life—and we've both been blessed with the opportunity to rescue Cynthia's life as well."

"You deserve it."

Delbert successfully retracted flaps and climbed to three thousand feet, then turned back over the lake. He brought power back to idle and allowed the airplane to slow into a stall. He was apprehensive about the first stall, not knowing how it would react. At forty-six knots the nose pitched down. He made a smooth recovery.

Next, he extended flaps and with power applied pulled the nose up until it stalled again. This time there was a violent pitch down. The rapid loss of altitude startled Sylvia as she watched from the ground. She decided it must be one of his tests when he recovered the lost altitude. She watched a little longer before leaving. *There's no one more capable of testing a new airplane. I have to have faith in him. I do have faith in him.*

In an hour Delbert was one with his aircraft. He understood exactly what it could do. He contacted air traffic control to test his radio. When he identified himself with the call letters he was assigned, CH-3394, the controller became curious.

"Say your name and describe your aircraft."

"Delbert Pillage. Three three niner four is a small flying boat of my own design."

"Delbert Pillager Pillage?"

"Affirmative but I don't pillage these days."

"Delbert, how about making a low pass by the tower and give us a look-see?"

"Roger. Departing Elk Lake now at three thousand."

"Our pattern is empty at the moment. Cleared for a pass at six hundred feet."

After he made the pass, the controller came on again.

"That's the weirdest looking rig we've ever seen. We've christened it the Delboat. That will be your identifier in future."

Delboat! Delboat…actually, it's not a bad name. Gives them a laugh anyway. He headed for Langford Lake.

Jim and Edith were sitting on the front porch when he taxied up to them. They had not heard him land and were surprised when he came in view. Like everyone else they thought it looked strange. Delbert opened the window and waved. He called to them.

"See how quiet it is. The engine is running right now. I'll takeoff and come back and land to see what you think."

He closed the window, turned to takeoff and applied power. The fans spun up and he was soon accelerating up the lake. In almost no time he reached sixty knots and lifted off. He turned and flew past their house at three hundred feet, then flew to the far end and turned to land toward them. When he stopped in front of the house, Jim had walked down onto the float.

"That's the damnedest thing I ever saw. All we could hear was what sounded like wind. You got some kind of magic technology there?"

"No magic. We just designed it to be silent."

"Well, we'd be proud to have a local hero park at our float."

"Would thirty dollars a month be acceptable?"

"That would be a nice little add-on to our pension but if it gets to be a burden on you, we'll let you moor free."

"Thirty dollars is a bargain for me."

Wonder if I can dock this thing by myself. He taxied in next to the float, threw the forward mooring line out through the window, unlatched his chair, rolled back and dropped the ramp/door. He threw out the aft mooring line and rolled down the ramp. His worst fear was that the plane would drift away. It did move out slightly before he collected the aft line and tied it off on a cleat.

Jim had picked up the forward line which he fastened to a second cleat on the float.

"Thanks. Think I better rig up lines on the float that I can hook onto with a pole and pull into the plane. Shouldn't leave it before it's moored."

"No. Wouldn't want your machine drifting around the lake."

Delbert's real concern involved the possibility of the ramp slipping off the float and dumping him in the water. It was nearly three hours since he first took off. Could he catch Sylvia at home and redirect her to the new location?

"Jim, would it be possible to use your phone and call my wife to pick me up here?"

"Sure. Come on."

Delbert followed him to the house. He stopped at the base of four steps to the porch. Jim recognized his problem and led him around to the front door on the road side. There was a single low step to the front porch which Delbert could back up over, another at the door. Jim showed him the phone. Sylvia answered.

"Where are you? Is everything okay?"

"I'm at the Brown's. They'll rent us their float. Can you come and get me here?"

"Sure. I was getting ready to head back to Elk Lake. I'll come right away."

"Better call Max first and let him know. Ask him if he will take the trailer back to our place. We won't need it for a while."

"Okay. See you soon."

Delbert thanked Jim and wheeled back to the float. He boarded the plane, checked everything and shut down all equipment. While it was fresh in his mind, he made notes of what he had learned throughout the morning such as stall speeds, optimum climb and cruise speeds and power settings, etc. Then he worked on checklists for each flight phase.

When Sylvia drove in, he wheeled down the ramp, lifted and locked it, checked the mooring lines and bumpers, then rolled up to meet her. She loved the happy, enthusiastic expression on his face.

"It's unbelievably good, honey. Tomorrow afternoon I want to take you up for a ride."

"Please take Max first. He did so much of the work he deserves to be the first passenger."

"Good idea. As a matter of fact, you could both come — there's two seats."

"I want to ride in it, but you should take him alone first, sort of special treatment." *I hope he doesn't think I'm afraid to fly in it.*

Chapter 40

Spring rapidly became Luke's worst season. As soon as he finished shearing sheep, it was time to plow and plant the vegetables. It irritated him that Jake drove the new tractor while he walked behind tossing seed potatoes into the plowed furrow.

Jake's acting like he owns the place when he's really a hired hand just like me. Thinks he's married but he aint. She gets tired of him and he'll be out on his ear. Wonder if they keep separate accounts. Wonder what his take is—bet it's more than twenty-five percent.

After a hard day's work, it galled him even more to milk the cow. The disparity between the work he and Jake faced ate at him. The worst part was the way it tired him out. Lettie wanted sex every night. He was often so tired he just wanted to sleep. Most nights she enticed him to participate anyway. But when she couldn't arouse him two nights in a row, she got mad and went back to the main house.

Jake felt her arrival first. He knew he should send her back, but the thrill of her company kept him quiet. Madge soon realized they had company.

"Lettie, what are you doing here?"

"Luke just wants to sleep. I got bored."

Later, Madge told her to go back to Luke.

"I want you in bed with him when he wakes up. If he finds out you've been with us, he may get mad and leave. Jealousy always causes trouble."

She reluctantly got up and left. Jake was sorry to see her go. Madge sensed that. It angered her.

"Damn it Jake, your greed gets the better of you. I've let you live here as though we are married, sharing everything. Maybe that's a mistake. Maybe I should have kept you a hired hand paid thirty-five percent of the drug money."

"Calm down Madge. This arrangement is good for you too. Without me the operation would have folded as soon as you shot Hank."

Why did he put it that way? Is he blackmailing me? Telling me he'd turn me in if I toss him out? It would be his word against mine about who shot him. Hell, we would both be guilty if it ever came out.

"I see how much work Luke does on the farm and how little you do. We can't afford to have him get fed up and leave."

He had to agree that made sense. "I'll try to even it out more."

"And send Lettie back to him if she shows up again."

"Okay."

* * *

Luke slept through Lettie's absence. Didn't know she had left. What he did notice was the change in Jake. They shared the workload more equally. Jake even milked the cow in the afternoon. Madge worked in the gardens, planting and weeding. They became a harmonious crew and it paid dividends for Luke and Lettie at night. A tongue lashing from Madge made it clear she was not welcome in their bed.

The drug runs ran so smoothly they became a little complacent. On the American delivery in the first week of June, they failed to notice a Coast Guard patrol boat round the point just west of their drop area. It was too close for them to slip the package overboard. Jake had no choice but to wheel around and race north. He ignored the Coast Guard siren. They fired a shot across his bow. He went into a zigzag path as additional shots landed closer.

"Christ, Jake they're trying to kill us!"

"I'm not spending the rest of my life in a U.S. jail."

At full speed and with random turns, he was not an easy mark for the Coast Guard gunner who had little experience shooting at moving targets. When the racer crossed into Canadian waters, he had to stop firing. Jake's first inclination was to duck into Sooke. *They'll call the B.C. police for sure. Better run for home.* He raced along the shoreline without running lights past Victoria in hopes he could get into the boathouse before they picked up the chase.

As they pulled into the boathouse, Luke scanned the strait. No sign of a patrol boat. They made it. He started to shake as post traumatic shock set in.

"Shit, that was too close."

"Luke, get that package up to the cave and don't use a light."

Jake tied up the boat and rushed to close the doors. He had to agree it was too close. They would have to change drop zones. *I'll call them tomorrow and take care of that. Better postpone the drop and paint the boat a different color. They'll be watching for this one now. Damn it, I should have been more alert. We've had it too good this Spring.*

Madge was surprised when he walked in. "That was a quick drop."

"No drop. The Coast Guard caught us and fired a shot across our bow before we could ditch the package."

"How did you get away?"

"Outran them. Luke's stashing it back in the cave."

"What happens now?"

"Hank figured they would eventually get a picture of us. We repaint the boat black with the paint he stored in the shed."

"Cover up that beautiful wood hull?"

"That's right. Use the little boat to take Lettie to school from now on. And I need it to run into Sydney tomorrow."

"She only has another week and a half."

* * *

Jake lay on the foredeck and reached down to paint the hull above the waterline stripe. It was agonizing work in this position. He had to get up and rest every ten minutes. Luke had an easier time standing in the rear leaning over the coaming. It was slow, painful work. They reminded each other it was the price to pay for continued operation.

Jake had called his American contact and arranged a new drop point a week later. The plan now was to hug the coastline all the way to Port Renfrew, hide there until dark and make a quick run across to Snow Creek on tribal lands. It would be considerably less risky.

It took three days to repaint the boat, another to touch up missed spots and paint a new name on the transom. And fake registration numbers. The boat's rebirth was complete in time for the delivery, which went off without a hitch. Their only serious exposure to authorities occurred during the daylight run to Port Renfrew. This delivery point appealed to Jake; however, he now understood the need to vary the location in future.

Chapter 41

Delbert spent time in the air almost every day. He soon had sufficient confidence in Delboat to take the others up. Each was thrilled with the experience, especially Cynthia.

After arranging a time and place to meet with Dan and Jack, he flew to Vancouver to pick them up. Dan was the first to control flight from the right seat. He was delighted with its flight characteristics though it took some time to get used to controlling the rudder with the secondary joystick.

"I automatically push with my foot when I enter a turn."

Delbert teased, "Welcome to the footless world. That was pretty sloppy, by the way."

Meanwhile, Jack constantly scrutinized gages. He detected no faults.

With joyride obligations fulfilled, he turned his attention to patrol activity. *Where do I start? What's my goal even? Jesse Thompson thinks they come in by sea. Probably from the Orient by ship. They must pass them to someone local for distribution. Could be after docking. Can't do anything in that case. But if the transfer is made at sea to a small boat I could help. Need to find a way to detect it. At least that's a starting point.*

He spent a full day just flying the waters northwest from Victoria. The shipping lanes were easily identified. *A ship that deviated from these lanes to make a drop would be suspicious. The drop must occur in the lanes—if there is a drop.* For the next five afternoons he flew coastlines. He cataloged in his mind every place that could harbour a small boat. Sylvia sometimes joined him. It reminded her of their first flight together.

On weekends, Cynthia wanted to go with him. She disproved his feeling that she would soon tire of long hours in the air. It seemed like an opportunity to teach her to fly and she proved to be a quick learner with good coordination. In fact, she reminded him of his early hours in the air with Dan. Within a month she became a competent pilot from takeoff through landing. She loved it.

Delbert bought her a logbook to record her flight time and a copy of the Private Pilot's Study Guide to learn the theory needed for a pilot's license. It was accompanied with a strong admonition to not neglect her school work.

"I have all week for that," she laughed.

"Teaching you to fly is a productive use of Delboat but we've made no progress on smuggler detection. Seems pretty hopeless."

"Don't you think they operate at night?"

Delbert paused. "You're right."

He altered his schedule to takeoff late in the afternoon, then realized he had never landed Delboat at night. Landing on a dark lake was far different from a lighted runway with electronic guidance available. *What if I can't see well enough to land? Stay in the air until dawn? One thing for sure, I'll try it by myself.*

He persuaded Sylvia to drop him off at the lake just after ten in the evening. With a full gas tank, he could stay aloft for over ten hours if necessary. He taxied out on the lake and turned on the landing lights. They were angled down into the water less than a hundred feet in front. Jack did that on purpose to compensate for the airplane attitude on approach.

Well, here goes. He turned off the landing lights and took off. He could barely make out the shoreline in what little moonlight existed. House lights outlined the boundaries somewhat. He circled at a thousand feet and set up the approach. The hard part would be judging his height above the water. He turned on the landing lights and descended cautiously with landing flaps.

The water became visible in the lights, but he still couldn't measure height. The answer was to arrest the sink rate and feel his way down. He gaged the distance left on the lake and was about to abort the landing when splashdown occurred. He decelerated quickly. It worked. There was room to spare.

I need to be careful here at the lake. Any less moonlight would make it impossible. However, I could land on the sea and drift around until lighting improves. Or stay aloft. Think it's safe enough for night patrols. Do I let Thia come along? She'll want to for sure.

He took off again and spent the night flying up and down the shipping lanes studying the boats and watching for anything unusual. He spotted nothing. Sylvia quizzed him when she picked him up in the morning.

"Is it really safe to fly at night?"

"Flying is no problem. Landing is the tricky part, especially on the lake."

"I wish you wouldn't do it then."

"There's safe alternatives when moonlight is insufficient. I can either stay aloft or land on the ocean and drift until dawn."

Sylvia sighed. "Do you think you'll ever find them?"

"Don't know, honey, but I enjoy the hunt."

"I don't enjoy the nights alone."

"That's a problem. Will you let me try this for a week or so?"

"Yes, if you promise not to fall asleep the minute we get home."

"That's a promise I desperately want to keep. Starting this morning."

* * *

Saturday promised a full moon. Cynthia pleaded to go. He agreed since it would be an opportunity to introduce her to night flying. Sylvia dropped them off at one in the afternoon with a promise to return at midnight. After a short flight to the gas dock in the inner harbour, they were in the air on a path that would take them up the east side of the Gulf Islands.

Cynthia flew at two thousand feet across the south end of Salt Spring Island.

"Wow. That black boat is really moving along."

"Where?"

"Ten o'clock low."

He chuckled at her terminology and spotted the boat.

"That's one of those speedboats they used to race before hydroplanes were invented. Bet it can go even faster than that."

He watched it round Isabella Point.

"Strange. Expected it to head to Victoria. It's turning up the strait. Swing around and follow it for a bit."

Cynthia brought the airplane around in a gentle turn and flew up the middle of the channel. They watched it slow, turn into a small bay and creep into a boathouse. She swung back for a closer look.

"That's Musgrave's Landing. It was quite a community at one time. Gradually everyone left except for the Smith family. Then they left too. Don't know who owns it now, probably squatters."

"Why would they have that speedboat?"

"Probably to get supplies, mail and things like that. There's no road to the farm."

Cynthia resumed their flight up the east side of the Gulf Islands. She's become a smooth pilot. Probably could pass the test for a private license if she had instrument and night flying hours. Think I'll let her shoot some landings after dark.

By early evening they covered the shipping lane right out to the open Pacific Ocean and were now flying back along it. They hoped to spot some interaction between a ship and small craft. They saw nothing suspicious.

It remained light after sunset, first from reflected sunlight, later by the rising moon.

"The water is fairly calm, Thia. Set up an approach and land in Comox Bay."

"Do you care which direction I land in?"

"I sure do. You know you always land into the wind."

"How do you know which way it's blowing out here?"

"Look for white caps if there are any, study the wave movement if not and if there are only ripples watch which way they move. You can land any way you want if it's flat calm. If it's too dark to see anything, you just have to guess and be ready to go around if it looks wrong near the water."

Cynthia correctly determined the proper approach direction and set up a gentle descent. Delbert instructed her how to land without depth perception. He had her make three landings and takeoffs before heading home.

Landing at Langford Lake after dark was much trickier. Flat, calm water provided no depth perception. Lights in houses around the lake helped a little. Yet the surface could be one foot or two hundred feet down.

"Dad, I can't judge the height at all."

"Stay calm. Assume you are about to touch down at any instant and set up the appropriate sink rate. The thing to watch is how much lake you have left to decelerate. When it gets close, do a go-around and try again."

"Will we splash down hard?"

"Not too hard. The ground effect close to the water will slow the descent."

"Think you want it to be water effect here." Both laughed.

She felt the slight increase in lift and almost immediately the hull hit the water, skipped and settled back down when she pulled the power back.

"Good job. Now let's get it stopped."

She already had the water jet extended and was ramping up the pump to get reverse thrust. In a few minutes the float came in sight.

"That was excellent, Thia. No pilot I know could have done better."

"Except the one you know best?"

"Even him." She felt a glow of pride.

Sylvia waited on the float to tie the mooring lines. While Delbert shut everything down, Cynthia ducked under the engine inlet and opened the ramp door. Delbert wheeled out and Cynthia closed and locked the door.

"Did you two find anything?"

"No. Cynthia became a proficient night flier though."

Chapter 42

"I'm bored."

Less than two weeks out of school and Lettie was tired of cooking, tending chickens and weeding the garden. The stretch of days when she had to avoid sex didn't help.

She repeated, "I'm bored, Luke. I want to get off this damn farm and find some excitement. Maybe in Victoria."

"I can't leave, and Madge won't let you go."

"Maybe I won't tell her I'm leaving."

I can't let her do that. Don't want to let her go. There's a sure way to solve the problem if I can keep it secret from Madge and Jake.

"Honey, there's a way to give you an experience more exciting than anything you'll find in Victoria."

Skeptical, "Oh yeah, what's that?"

"We have to keep it secret from the others. They'd fire me or worse if they find out."

"Sounds interesting. What is it?"

"An injection that will give you a thrill wilder than anything you can imagine."

"You mean a fix. I don't want to become a junkie."

"With this stuff, you can take it or leave it. I've used it and you don't see me addicted."

"Are you sure?"

"Sure. We can do it together. You'll see. But we've got to stay in here until it wears off. Let's do it this evening."

"I'll try it once."

As he had done before, Luke cut some heroin six to one with sugar and made a second bag with pure sugar. After dinner, he brought out two syringes, wiped two spoons with alcohol and poured in the real and fake heroin mixtures. He drew the correct amount of water into each syringe and squirted it into the spoons. After warming and stirring the liquid, he drew it back into the syringes.

"Do yours first."

He injected the sugar solution into a vein in his arm. She held out her arm, excited by the anticipation of a new experience. He injected the heroin and told her to lie down. He crossed and latched the door, then lay down beside her.

The high came quickly for her. At first she laughed and hugged him. He laughed with her. Gradually the euphoria transported her into another world. He watched her, the effect was exactly what he wanted, a strong high but short of an overdose.

She awoke with a slight headache in the morning. It barely dimmed her memory of the ecstasy felt the night before. She thanked Luke with a passionate kiss and almost succumbed to sex before she remembered it was a bad time.

"Let's do it again tonight, Luke."

"I'll fix one for you, Let, I better hold off or Jake will bark at me for not getting my work done. You need to take care of your chores too."

A routine developed. Each night Luke would give her a fix. On the third night, he wanted sex first. In anticipation of the high, she was more passionate than ever, even though it was still too early in the month. Sex became an integral part of the pattern. He made sure she continued to look after the chickens and work in the garden. She showed no outward sign of her growing addiction. In fact, a relieved Madge only noticed they had grown close again.

Luke ran into an unanticipated problem when the next pick up night rolled around. Lettie's addiction now demanded a daily fix. Since he and Jake would leave about six, it would be too early for her. Not only that, she and Madge made a habit of spending the evening together when the men were gone.

"You will have to skip tonight, Let."

"I can't."

Damn it. What am I going to do? If I cook the fix in the afternoon, she'll probably inject as soon as we leave.

"If I make up a shot for you, can you leave it alone until you come back from talking to Madge?"

"Sure, anything you say."

"I don't believe you."

"I will, honest I will. I'll go over and talk to Mum like always. Just knowing it's there when I get back is enough."

He was reluctant but saw no better alternative. He cooked her shot and showed where he put it in the cupboard. She looked longingly at the needle.

"Promise me you won't let Madge find out. If she does, it will be the last fix you get from me."

"I promise." She kissed him before he joined Jake.

All through dinner and wine with Madge, her thoughts were on the needle. She wanted to get through their little ritual as soon as possible. As Madge finished washing dishes, Lettie forced herself to be calm and chat as they usually did. At eight, Lettie said she had to get some sleep.

"Why dear? The men won't be home for hours."

"I need a good night's sleep for a change."

Madge let her leave. She could hardly wait to grasp the needle and inject the fix. She was stoned in a trance when Luke returned. He assumed it went alright since Madge was not ranting at him. Still, he didn't like the added risk of discovery.

Chapter 43

Sylvia decided to counter evening loneliness by joining the daily expeditions. She sat in the back seat as an observer. The quiet craft facilitated conversation. At times, they felt they should whisper to not be overheard outside, then laugh at their absurdness. It became a pleasant family outing.

"Look, Dad, there's that black boat again, heading up the narrows."

"What's so special about the black boat?" Sylvia asked.

"Nothing special. It's an old race boat owned by the people at Musgrave's Landing."

"Smiths?"

"They're gone now. I think the farm's run by squatters these days."

"He's not moving very fast."

"They're impressive boats. Take us down for a closer look."

Cynthia descended to two hundred feet above the water and approached them from behind. As she drew abreast, they became aware of the strange airplane and turned to study it. Cynthia suddenly banked sharply to the left, her face as white as a sheet.

"What's the matter, Thia?"

"Luke. That was Luke in the boat."

* * *

"What the hell kind of plane was that?"

"Never seen one before. Didn't hear it coming even though we're not making much noise. He peeled off the minute we saw him. I don't like it."

"You watch behind for him. If he comes back, we'll chase him. Pretend it's a race and get a good look at the pilot. Also, memorize his call letters."

* * *

"Are you sure it was Luke?"

"Ninety percent sure."

"Was he driving?"

"No, the other one was."

"Perhaps we should get a look at them through the binoculars."

"No," Sylvia said firmly, "stay away for today at least. If they're smugglers, we've already made them suspicious."

"Sure would like to know where they're going. Looked like they might head up into the Strait of Georgia and that connects with the shipping lane."

"Or they could be on their way to Campbell River. We should give them a wide berth anyway."

"You're right, Sylvia. We could do that by flying around the east side of the strait to Sechelt. I know a good bay to park in just west of there. We could watch for them with the binoculars from out of sight."

"They might have binoculars too."

"They would never spot us and we can takeoff away from them if necessary. They can't chase us over land."

Sylvia acquiesced against her better judgment. They flew a circuitous path to Sechelt and landed in Delbert's bay. He kept the plane pointed east while the two women scanned the horizon. They waited half an hour.

"That boat should be in sight by now. Perhaps he went in to Nanaimo."

"Let's give them a little more time. They were not in any hurry."

Cynthia interrupted. "I think I see it. Look, Mum, right in front of the highest peak."

"It's just a black speck…it could be them."

Ten minutes later they were fairly certain it was the black boat. It moved in the direction of the islands to their west. They followed its progress, ready to takeoff at a moment's notice if it veered toward them. But it held its course. They watched it disappear into Lasqueti Island. Delbert taxied behind the point of the bay to ponder their next step out of sight.

"I think we're on to something. Maybe they went on up but I don't think they would use that route if they were going to Campbell River, certainly not for Comox or Courtenay. And the ships come right by here on their way to Vancouver."

"You think they are here to pick up a drug shipment?"

"It's a definite possibility. I'm going to taxi across the bay just in case they did somehow spot us. Don't think for a minute that they did but if they came roaring around the point we would still have time to get away."

"What good does it do to sit in the bay?" Sylvia asked.

"We might see a transfer even from this distance and after dark, we can get closer."

Sylvia was not enthused. Cynthia was torn between fear of Luke and excitement of the hunt. They settled into the boredom of waiting for action. Each ship that passed received scrutiny. Delbert copied down names and times. Darkness came slowly. When it made viewing Lasqueti impossible through the binoculars, Delbert turned off their navigation lights and taxied out of the bay to where they could still read the ship names.

Suddenly there was a light signal from the island, short-long-short. The passing ship answered with a brief flash.

"It is a drop," Delbert whispered. "What's the ship's name?"

"Titan Maru."

Delbert turned off all lights in the cockpit and taxied toward the ship's path.

"Be careful," Sylvia cautioned.

"I will."

Five minutes passed. *Where's the black boat? It will be invisible now. Probably trailing the ship. Have to stay clear.* His thoughts were interrupted by two brief flashes from the ship. *That must be the drop signal.* They waited. Above the steady throb of the big ship's propellers, they heard another boat. Delbert backed away to put more distance between them.

A flashlight came on. *They're searching for the drop. Don't shine it this way.* He wanted to increase the reverse speed but it might kick up a telltale fluorescent wake. All three were silent, each with similar thoughts. Delbert estimated they were a quarter mile from the searchers. *Is that enough?*

The flashlight swung toward them. *They're doubling back. Keep that light pointed down.* They obliged by pointing it into the water. *The pick up!* The light flashed up across them, then went out. *Did they spot us?*

* * *

"I think I saw a boat over there."

"There's no lights."

"Quick. Get the sugar fastened on. I want to take a look. Be ready to dump them overboard if I give the word."

The engine roared to life and Jake made a high-speed beeline north.

* * *

"There's a wake! Looks like they're coming this way!"

Delbert was already applying power. *I'm going all the way to maximum thrust.* The flashlight came on and spotlighted the airplane.

Sylvia screamed, "They're almost on us. They're going to ram us."

Delbert remained calm as possible, "They won't damage their boat."

In the panic it seemed to take forever to reach sixty knots. He was tempted to rotate early in hopes it would lift off. Cynthia reached over and selected takeoff flaps. *Damn, how could I forget that? Almost sixty knots.* He raised the nose. They were airborne. A second later the boat roared under them in a turn to match their course.

Delbert banked the other way. The boat made a sweeping turn toward him. It kept up with them. Delbert glanced at his airspeed. A hundred and thirty knots! He turned again and headed toward the shoreline. Another twenty knots faster, he was pulling away. Once over land, he turned to find the boat. It was gone.

A wake was soon visible, headed south. All three breathed again.

"Thanks Thia."

"For what?" He tapped the flap selector.

She nodded. "They're making a high-speed run for home."

Sylvia had enough excitement. "Let's stay here until they are long gone."

Delbert mentally calculated how long the run would take at their speed. He would have to turn south soon if he wanted to verify their destination. They might be headed directly to a delivery point. It was too good an opportunity to let slip away.

"It's safe to move now."

He turned on the lights and gained altitude down the east side of the islands. He planned to cross behind them at three thousand feet. He could watch them from a distance—if he could spot the boat again.

That proved easy. The fast boat's wake was clearly visible from the air. He didn't like the fact that the moon was rising, however, the chance of detection would remain remote as long as he didn't cross in front of it.

Cynthia piped up. "The wake is disappearing. They must have slowed down."

"That's close to Musgrave's Landing. They take the drugs back there before delivery."

* * *

Luke picked up the drug packages while Jake buttoned up the boat.

"Another good night's work, Luke. Want me to carry one of those?"

"I can manage. What do you make of that damn plane?"

"Don't like it one bit. It was the same one we saw earlier. Didn't see any official markings on it. Maybe some nosy bastard. From now on we carry a rifle in the boat. He comes around again we shoot him down."

Luke scanned the horizon before starting up the path. He noticed airplane navigation lights moving south.

"Funny, I didn't hear that one go by."

"Where?" Jake turned to follow Luke's point.

"Could be anyone. Or it could be him. He has to be moored somewhere around the bottom end of the Island. I'll go look for it on Saturday. Find out who owns it."

Chapter 44

On Saturday, Jake set off in the racer after morning chores. He found no sign of any seaplane until he entered Victoria's inner harbour. The few moored there didn't resemble the one he was after. Nor did one found in the Gorge. Continuing on around the coast as far as Sooke turned up nothing. *Maybe it's an amphibian and they park it at the airport.*

Jake docked at Sydney and found a taxi to take him across to the airport. A scan of light aircraft parked around the terminal indicated it was either not there or parked in a hangar. He entered the terminal and located the weather office. An old man behind the counter asked if he wanted to file a flight plan.

"No. Actually, I'm looking for a very interesting plane I saw yesterday. Trying to find out what it is."

"What did it look like?"

When he described it, the man shook his head.

"Doesn't sound like anything here at the field. You sure it's an amphibian rather than a flying boat, say."

"It probably is a flying boat."

"Well, it wouldn't be here then. Must be moored on water—ocean or lake."

"Which lakes?"

"Elk, Thetis, both kind of small and crowded. Shawnigan Lake would be a good candidate or perhaps Langford."

Armed with his clues, he told the driver to take him to Elk Lake. After driving around it, he moved on to Thetis. No luck at either. Langford was next although he began to think it would take the long drive to Shawnigan Lake.

Although fairly well sheltered from public access, Delboat could be seen from the road in front of the Brown's house. And it was.

"Stop! That's it. Wait here."

Jim Brown answered the door.

"Noticed your seaplane down there. It's sure unusual. What kind is it?"

"It's a home-built, one of a kind."

"You build it?"

"Heck no. I know nothing about flying, much less building an airplane."

"Whose is it? I would sure like to talk to the man who designed it."

"Delbert Pillage designed and built it." Jim said it with a tone that implied he expected everyone to know the name.

"Can you give me his address or phone number?"

Jim became wary, "No, don't have them. He just drops by when he takes the plane out."

Jake sensed he would get nothing further so he thanked him. Delbert Pillage is an unusual name. Should be able to find him.

"Let's head back to town."

Two hours later Sylvia parked by the float. Jim saw them and came out.

"Delbert, somebody was here earlier looking at your plane. Said he wanted to know what it was. When I told him it was a home-built, he wanted to know your name. Think he wants to learn more about it."

"You gave him my name?"

"Yeah, was that wrong?"

"I prefer to keep it secret as much as possible. Don't want vandals or reporters nosing around."

"Wish I hadn't given it to him now. He wanted a phone number and address, but I played dumb on that."

* * *

Sylvia waited until they were airborne.

"Do you think it was them?"

"Pretty unlikely."

He thought the opposite but refused to alarm her. It seemed prudent to steer clear of Musgrave's Landing today. He decided to drop into Ganges and talk with Cal or Mattie.

Cal was in the police station.

"Captain, I want to bring you up to speed on something we've uncovered."

He described the transfer they witnessed. Cal was in favor of obtaining a search warrant and investigating the landing.

"The drugs will be gone by the time you get there. And you can't sneak in by boat. We need to catch them the day after a drop to find the drugs in their possession."

"What's your suggestion for doing that?"

"I suspect the drops are fairly regular. This one was made by the Titan Maru. We should track the shipping news and watch for ships in the Maru line. When we spot a transfer, I'll call you. I can fly you and Mattie into a small cove west of the landing."

"We don't want to put you in danger."

"We will be out of sight from the farm."

"Well, if you're game to do that, I'll get a search warrant ready and wait for your call."

Chapter 45

Delbert wasn't surprised when Sylvia voiced her concern later. He placated her.

"They have some danger to deal with, but I will be safe."

He would be far closer to harm than she wanted. And her fear escalated Sunday mid-morning. After she returned from mass, Delbert set off on his exercise circuit. Moments later the doorbell rang. The man in front of her arrived in a taxi parked on the street.

"Mrs. Pillage?"

"Yes." Her concern mounted.

"I'm Larry Smith. Could I please talk to Delbert?"

"Afraid you just missed him."

"Was that him in the wheelchair?"

"Yes," she replied reluctantly.

"Oh, the Delbert Pillage I'm looking for flies a seaplane he built. Do you know any other Delbert Pillages here in town?"

"No...although there must be one. A few months ago, we had a phone call from someone trying to find him."

He appeared disappointed. "Sorry to bother you."

After he left, she started shaking. There was no doubt that the enemy had now shown up at their doorstep. She sat down at the kitchen table. A tear formed in each eye.

Cynthia sensed her anxiety. She put a hand on her shoulder.

"That was quick thinking, Mum. It threw him off track."

"It won't be long before he finds out Delboat is piloted from a wheelchair."

"He did look like the other man in the boat but how will he connect Dad with Delboat?"

"By watching who comes and goes."

Delbert returned to find Sylvia in tears, Cynthia comforting her.

"What happened? What's the matter?"

Sylvia answered, "They've found us."

Cynthia described the unwelcome visit. Delbert wheeled into their bedroom and reappeared five minutes later with his service revolver in his lap.

"Drive me over to the shooting range in Saanich. I need to brush up on my marksmanship and buy ammunition."

"Or we could hide in a motel up island."

"No. We've come this far and are very close to putting them out of business. We need to see it through for the sake of all the people whose lives will be destroyed if we don't."

"What about our lives?"

"We can protect ourselves."

Sylvia remained unconvinced but argument was pointless. Cynthia oscillated between their two sides.

* * *

"I found that airplane. It's moored on Langford Lake. Built by a guy named Delbert Pillage."

"He used to live here on the island. Got hurt in a plane crash. He's a paraplegic now."

"He couldn't be the one we're after, can't pilot an airplane from a wheelchair. I talked to that one's wife. She says there's another guy with the same name in Victoria somewhere."

"Well, he was a test pilot."

"From what little I know about flying, a paraplegic can't push rudder pedals or brake the plane after landing."

"There's no brakes on a seaplane."

After a pause, "Maybe it is him. Perhaps she was trying to throw me off. But she wouldn't know I'm the one he's watching."

"You might want to go back."

"Yeah. Wouldn't hurt to give them a phone call scare when I'm in town. We've got to look after those lambs before the next run. I'll take care of him after that unless he comes snooping around again."

* * *

Delbert rolled to the ringing phone and answered it.

"Delbert Pillage?" a gruff voice asked.

"Yes."

"Sticking your nose where it doesn't belong can get it shot off."

There was a click and the line went dead.

"Who was that?" Sylvia asked.

Reluctantly he confessed, "A phone threat."

"From them?"

"I assume so, unless it was just a crank call."

"You know it wasn't a crank call. What are we going to do?"

"It was a warning to stay away. From now on we will do that—stay out of sight. We're too close to ending their operation to give up now."

"Unless they end ours first."

He paused to rethink the situation. It wasn't right to put them at risk.

"Perhaps you two should go stay with my folks until this blows over."

"No, I'm not leaving you here alone. How would you get around? You can't be constantly calling for taxi's."

"I can manage."

"No! We're in this together, for better for worse."

"Well, Thia, maybe you should visit them for a while."

"No way, Dad! I won't leave either. You may need a co-pilot. Besides, I'm like Mum. I want to stick with you two no matter what happens."

"How did I get saddled with two stubborn women?"

"Not saddled, dear…blessed."

"Yes."

Chapter 46

The shipping news in the Vancouver Sun listed all ships moored plus their scheduled departures. It also provided scheduled arrivals. Delbert checked each day. The Titan Maru stayed for four days, then departed for San Francisco. It wouldn't show up again for at least a month.

A week later, the Osan Maru appeared on the schedule. It would arrive in Vancouver the following Thursday. Delbert called Cal to alert him.

Wednesday afternoon, Delbert, Cynthia and Sylvia took off and flew to Swartz Bay. They landed just out of view of Musgrave's Landing and taxied to a position that barely let them watch it through binoculars. While Sylvia scanned the shoreline, Delbert kept the plane in position.

"They would need a telescope to spot us here."

"I hope so," Sylvia responded. "I don't like this."

"Don't worry, Mum, we can outrun them if they chase us."

"How do you know? Their boat is faster than ours."

Delbert signaled Cynthia to keep quiet and responded, "Not when we're airborne."

"What makes you think they will pick up drugs today?"

"It's just a guess. It stands to reason that the rendezvous would be after dark or at least at dusk. That's about when the Osan Maru is scheduled to enter the straits. Who knows, we may be doing this for days."

* * *

Jake kept Luke busy with fence repairs until it was time to leave. He had no chance to prepare a fix for Lettie.

"You'll have to hold on until we get back."

"I can't. I need it now."

"Calm down. Tell Madge you feel sick and stay in here. Do it, Lettie. You have to keep our secret or there won't be any more."

She cried when he left. Then pulled herself together and crossed to the main house.

"Mum, I feel sick. Think I'm getting the flu. I'm going to bed."

"Don't you want something to eat first?"

"No, I'm too queasy to eat."

Back in the cottage, she hunted for Luke's stash. She could cook her own fix after watching him go through the process. *Where does he hide it?* Her frustration grew as she ransacked the cottage. She finally found a small package in a dusty old boot in the back of the storeroom.

Quickly, she went through the steps he did. Excited now in anticipation of the high, she hurried around tidying up the cottage again. She could do it afterwards but thought Luke might return too soon. When everything was neat, she eagerly returned to the bed. In case Madge checked in on her, she undressed and climbed under the covers. Then she injected his uncut heroin into a vein and hid the syringe.

The euphoria came quickly. Too quickly. Not like before. A tremor of fear crossed her mind. Her pulse slowed. Breathing became shallow. Pain signals from her body cried for oxygen and were ignored. Her eyes took on an expression of terror. Some part of her brain registered a panic awareness of the spreading numbness and increasing cold. It fought for recognition. Nothing responded. A blank curtain slowly descended over her eyes. The last thing she sensed was the mocking screech of a seagull somewhere down on the beach.

* * *

The hours dragged by. They took turns with the binoculars. Around six Sylvia asked if they were getting hungry. She preferred to leave the area.

"There's the black boat." Cynthia cried.

"Which way is it going?"

"Away."

Delbert taxied back out of sight and waited to give them a head start.

"What are you going to do now?"

"In a little while we'll take off and fly up the far side of Salt Spring to spot where they are headed."

"Can you keep out of sight?"

"Yes, dear. Don't worry."

"Someone needs to worry for you."

"We've tracked them before, Mum."

"That doesn't fill me with confidence."

It was time to go after them. Delbert took off to the north across the south end of Salt Spring Island. He climbed along the east side of the island. *The higher we are the harder it will be for them to spot us.* He levelled off at six thousand feet on an intercept course. Cynthia and Sylvia scanned the water through binoculars. No luck. He turned further west.

"There they are, heading northwest past Gabriola."

"I'm going to cross behind them. Tell me if they appear to spot us or make any maneuvers."

Delbert continued over the Vancouver Island shoreline in a direction diverging from theirs. Cynthia and Sylvia now had a good view of the racer and reported it was on a steady course.

"They're not moving very fast."

"Probably so they won't attract attention."

Delbert was soon too far ahead of them. He flew a slow circle away from them. When they came in view again, Cynthia said they were headed into the little bay on that island.

"Lasqueti Island, Squitty Bay," Delbert said. "They must hole up there to wait for the drop. I'm going to get down low and land on this side of the island out of sight."

"Make sure you can get away if they come after us."

"I will."

After landing, he taxied to a point where they could barely see the mouth of Squitty Bay. They kept an eye out for approaching boats. A number of large ships passed the far side of the island in both directions. Delbert scanned each through binoculars. Nothing suspicious. Dusk approached. A freighter heading south caught his attention. It had three lights in an unusual triangular pattern.

"The boat came out," Sylvia said alarmed.

Delbert immediately taxied behind the island out of view. *Did they spot me? Need to pick up some speed for takeoff in case they come after us.* He increased engine speed and was soon skipping across the water to the north. *What do I do now? Climb back to altitude, then circle back.* He took off and climbed to the north.

"Can you see them back there?"

"Turn a little to the right." He complied.

"I see them. Looks like they're trailing the freighter. It just flashed a light twice."

He turned away again. "That's the drop signal."

He turned southeast at five thousand feet with navigation lights off. Strictly illegal, it bothered him, but he couldn't risk being spotted. In the encroaching darkness, he was sure they couldn't see him as long as he didn't cross in front of the moon. He could tell Sylvia was nervous and assured her they were safe.

"It's getting too dark to see them," Cynthia reported. "Wait. They're making a wake I can see now."

"They've got the drugs."

Delbert could now see their trail with his naked eye. He sped up in chase. It looked as if they were headed home. Still, they might stop somewhere else. He had to be sure. Faster than the racer in the air, he throttled back to match their speed.

"Are you sure they can't see us?"

"Not a chance in this darkness."

When they saw the wake die out near Musgrave's Landing, Delbert flew a large circle to the far side of the strait while Sylvia and Cynthia strained through binoculars to see anything at the landing. He continued the circle around behind Mount Toam and across the strait south of them again. On the second pass, both women reported seeing a light coming down the hill behind the landing.

"They cache the drugs somewhere up there. We can leave now and let the police know."

Sylvia was relieved to get away. Delbert contemplated his next move on the way home.

* * *

Luke knew something was wrong the instant he entered the cottage. It was too quiet. She should be anxiously waiting for him. He found her dead on the bed. *Lettie, what have you done? Christ, what have you done?* He found the needle and packet. *She used pure heroin! Lettie...Lettie.*

He held her in his arms and kissed her. It was like kissing a statue. For the first time in his adult life he found himself crying. He spent a sleepless night huddled with her.

Sometime toward morning he accepted that she was gone and began to think of himself again. *What do I do now? They'll kill me. Have to figure something out. Take what money I can and run. No. Heroin. Has to be just before we make the Victoria delivery. Shoot Jake. Give Madge an opportunity to throw in with me. Kill her too if not. Take twenty kilos and make a run to the States and get lost in the cities.*

I can cash in the heroin in San Francisco or L.A., then find a way to get to South America and live like a king. Hope Madge decides to take Lettie's place. Sex would be just as good, maybe better.

What if they insist on checking up on Lettie during the day? Then I'll have to move the schedule up.

Chapter 47

Early in the morning, Delbert phoned the Salt Spring police station. Cal answered.

"Captain, Delbert Pillage here. I'm ninety-nine percent sure there's currently drugs to be found at Musgrave's Landing. We watched them pick up a drop last night and stash it somewhere up behind their farm."

"We're ready to go."

"I'll pick you up at the seaplane dock in an hour."

"Got room for two in your plane?"

"Yes."

"Mattie and I will be waiting."

* * *

Sylvia and Cynthia insisted on going with him. Cal and Mattie stared at the airplane as it taxied in to the Ganges dock, then looked at each other with raised eyebrows. They held the strange looking craft while Sylvia and Cynthia stepped out onto the dock.

"What kind of airplane is this?" Mattie asked.

Delbert replied, "I designed it to be quiet, so it looks a little unconventional."

"A little? Will it get off the water with us? Thanks to Cal we weigh about twice as much as your girls."

Delbert laughed. "Don't worry. It will be the quickest and safest flight you will ever enjoy."

"As long as it's not too quick," she smiled as she climbed onboard.

He left the two women on the dock in exchange for the two officers and said he would come right back for them. Sylvia made him promise to stay out of sight of the landing. The airplane lifted off as advertised and set off across the island.

He flew in low from the north, landed close to the shore and taxied to the little cove as planned. Cal and Mattie jumped off, closed the door and splashed onto the beach. Delbert immediately taxied a quarter mile to the north and took off. The two women climbed on board when he docked in Ganges.

"How did it go?"

"Fine. They're hiking to the farm now. We better monitor from a distance in case they need help."

"What help can we give?"

"We can call Victoria police if necessary."

He took off and directly crossed the island to pass well northwest of the landing. Then he decided a closer look was needed and swung the airplane to make a pass down the channel. He caught a glimpse of either Cal or Mattie as they hiked along the slope toward the landing. Then he focused on the landing itself as it came into view. Two men stood in front of the main house facing the water, probably watching him. *The distraction might prove worthwhile.*

* * *

"How's Lettie?"

"She vomited during the night. Says she just wants to be left alone today. Hey, there's that plane again."

Jake raised his binoculars and scanned until he found it.

"He's watching us. I don't like it, even with the packages hidden in the cave. Get the rifles. It's time for a crash."

They ran inside and returned with rifles. Delbert was about two hundred yards from shore when they raised their guns and began to fire. A number of shots missed but finally a bullet penetrated the side panel, hit the wheelchair axle and deflected into Delbert's leg. The left side of the wheelchair collapsed dropping him down a foot.

"Thia! Get us out of here!"

A second bullet struck Delbert's forehead before exiting the right side in front of Cynthia.

Sylvia screamed, "Delbert!" His head was thrown back and blood poured from it. Cynthia banked the airplane hard to fly directly away from the landing. Sylvia crawled across behind Delbert. *Is he dead? So much blood.*

Frantic, she tore off her blouse and wrapped it around his head. The blood soaked through, but the flow ebbed. She could see blood on his left leg. It didn't look bad. Perhaps an advantage of poor circulation.

Delbert groaned. "What...happened?"

"You were shot. In the leg and forehead. It looks like you'll survive."

"Are we out of range?"

Cynthia answered, "Yes. I'm going to swing back around to see what's happening."

"No, we need to get Delbert to a hospital."

"I'll be alright. We can't leave them stranded there."

"I'll stay out of range, Mum. You can watch them through the binoculars."

Sylvia reluctantly conceded Cal and Mattie might need help. She crawled back to her seat and fumbled for her binoculars.

* * *

Cal and Mattie heard the shots. They ran as fast as terrain permitted until the landing came in sight. Two men were firing at the departing airplane.

Mattie saw them first and shouted, "Police! Freeze!"

Both men spun around and fired at the new threat. The first shot hit her in the leg. She fell down the slope behind a large boulder. The second shot whistled through the space her body vacated. The two men started toward her. They didn't see Cal appear higher on the slope. He fired once at Luke who twisted around and fell over backwards. Before Jake located him, Cal fired again. The bullet slammed into Jake's chest. He staggered. Tried to raise his rifle. Slid to his knees and collapsed face down in the dirt.

Madge screamed from the door, "Jake! Lettie, stay inside!"

Her child protection instinct was months too late. She ran to Jake, picked up his rifle, spotted Cal and fired. The shot whined over his head.

"Madge! Drop the gun!"

She answered with a second shot that struck the tree in front of him. He aimed at the woman standing there, her dress blowing in the breeze. He couldn't pull the trigger.

Mattie yelled, "Shoot! Before she kills you."

Another bullet knocked a chunk of bark off the trunk. He crouched down behind the base.

"I can't shoot a woman."

Mattie slid down the slope to her rifle, then painfully pulled herself up behind the boulder. Slowly, she peered around it to find the woman who was still concentrating on the tree, waiting for Cal to show his head again. Mattie slowly brought the rifle up in front of her.

"Drop the gun, Madge!"

Madge spotted her, swung the rifle around and fired. The bullet ricocheted off the boulder over Mattie's head. She fired back. Madge flew back a couple of steps and crumpled to the ground.

"Are you hit bad, Mattie?"

"I'll live. She called to her daughter. She must still be in there."

All was quiet. "Cover me. I'll look for her."

"Be careful, Cal. She may have a gun and what the hell was that about not being able to shoot a woman?"

"I couldn't bring myself to do it."

"Well, remember I'm a woman the next time I make you mad."

"I never forget you're a woman."

"Wait until I get where there's a clear shot at both doors. And don't get between me and either one of them."

She bit her lip as she pulled her wounded leg after her down the slope to a new vantage point.

"Okay. Be careful."

Before he stepped into the clearing, Cal shouted, "We know you are in there. Come out with your hands up."

No answer. He repeated the command. Still no answer. He drew his revolver and slowly walked toward the main house at an angle which prevented a shot through door or windows. When he stood beside the door, he prodded it open with the rifle in his left hand and repeated the command. Still nothing.

Carefully, he peered around the door. No movement. He ducked inside and crouched. The room was empty. He moved methodically from room to room. When he reappeared in the doorway, he signaled to Mattie it was empty.

The cottage came next. Nothing in the first room. He crept to the bedroom door. Inside, he saw a body on the bed, the teenage girl. She stared at the ceiling in a trance, paid no attention when he crossed the room. Her face was cold and hard. She had no pulse.

He ran back to Mattie. "She's dead. Looks like an overdose. Let me see your leg."

"I've held some pressure on it to stop the bleeding. It hurts like hell."

"I'll find something to bandage it."

"Make sure they're all out of commission first."

That made sense. It took only a moment to determine one man and the woman were dead. The second man moaned in a slowly expanding pool of blood. Cal picked up both rifles and ran back into the house. He found an old first aid kit in what appeared to be a pantry. It would have to do.

Mattie cut her pants away from the wound. He applied a dressing and bandage. She flinched as he secured the bandage.

He muttered, "Half of the most beautiful legs in the world have been damaged."

"It'll grow back. In the meantime, just look at the other one." He kissed her.

"I better signal Delbert."

He stood up and waved his hands over his head. The airplane drifted on the water, hopefully not too far away to see his signal.

Chapter 48

"Cal's waving. They have control of the situation. There are three people down. I can't see Mattie."

Delbert said, "She might be hurt. Take us in, Thia."

Cynthia turned toward the landing and took off. She flew a few feet above the water and splashed down again in time to coast into the bay. With the window up, she maneuvered the jet pump to bring them to the dock on her side. She and Sylvia dropped the door to its horizontal position. Sylvia jumped out taking a mooring line with her. Then returned for the front one and tied it off to a second cleat.

The two women set off up the slope toward Cal. Cynthia suddenly stopped short.

"What's the matter, Thia?"

"It's Luke!"

She approached him slowly. He looked to be dying.

"Luke, you bastard! I hope you burn in Hell!"

His eyes turned, tried to focus on her.

"Cynthia?"

"Yes. Die, you bastard, die!"

He stared at her with eyes that slowly turned to glass. They no longer saw anything.

"Come on, Thia. Remind me some time to talk to you about forgiveness."

They crossed to Cal.

"Mattie's got a bullet wound in her leg. We need to get her to a hospital."

Sylvia bent over her and inspected the bandage. Mattie looked at her.

"Do you always prance around in only a bra?"

Sylvia laughed. "My blouse is wound around Delbert's head to control bleeding."

"Is he hurt bad?"

"I think he'll be alright. We need to get both of you to the hospital." She turned to Cal. "Can we move her to the airplane?"

"The big ox can carry me." When Cal picked her up, she gasped in pain.

"I'm sorry, honey. Can you make it?"

"Let's go."

Sylvia led the way. "Put her in the back seat. I'll stay here while Thia flies them to Victoria. Then she can come back and pick us up."

"How are you, Delbert?" Cal asked.

"Biggest problem is my broken chair. Silly fools shot me where I can't feel it. The second shot just grazed my forehead. Lots of blood and a miserable headache but nothing worse."

Cynthia climbed in, closed the door and they cast off the mooring lines.

"Be careful, Thia."

"I will," she replied as she started the jet pump to taxi out to clear water. Soon she had the engine running and accelerated the plane for takeoff. Cal and Sylvia watched it climb out and head south.

Cal searched Jake and Luke's pockets. He found the little book and guessed its importance. It could be used to track down people above and below in the chain if the experts handled it with care. *That would be a good job for Mattie if she were healthy. She'd find them.*

Cal had never shot a human being before. It seemed surreal, alien to everything he knew. He felt himself going into shock and sat down. Sylvia sensed his condition, went into the house and returned with a wet towel.

"Put this on the back of your neck. Perhaps you should lie down."

"I'm sorry. This is new to me. It happened so fast."

"You had no choice. They turned it into a case of self-defence."

She got him a glass of water.

"Thanks. I'll be back to normal soon. You might want to borrow a blouse from the woman."

She looked down and laughed, "Yes. I forgot."

Mostly dresses hung in the main bedroom closet, however there were a few blouses. She took one that went with her slacks. Out of curiosity she wandered through the house before leaving. In the den she noticed a suitcase in the middle of the room. *It's out of place.* She crossed and lifted it. Too heavy to be empty, she opened it to find stacks of American cash. *The woman planned to take off with the money.* She closed the suitcase and walked outside to tell Cal.

Then she entered the cottage and stopped short at the sight of the girl on the bed who stared unseeing at the ceiling. Sylvia knelt by the bed, tried to close Lettie's eyes unsuccessfully. She clasped a cold, hard hand between hers as if she could warm it, bring some life back into it. The thought that this could be Cynthia plagued her mind. Tears blinded her eyes and ran down her cheeks.

She thought that last rites should be administered but couldn't remember the words. She said a prayer for the girl's soul, then wondered why she prayed. Surely, a benevolent God wouldn't let this happen. The compassion she naturally felt for the dead adults outside dissipated when she thought of the tragic result of their greed. She understood Delbert's compulsion to fight them no matter the danger.

Chapter 49

Cynthia tuned the radio to 121.5, "Charlie hotel three three niner four declaring an emergency."

A voice came back, "Delboat, state your problem."

"We have two injured passengers. I'm taking them to Elk Lake. Can you have ambulances meet us at the public boat ramp?"

"Roger. Ambulances at the public ramp. Is that contraption operating normally?"

"As normal as it ever does."

She heard a chuckle. "Stay on this frequency. We'll monitor your progress."

"Roger. Wilco."

Delbert watched her with a wonderful feeling of pride. *She does a beautiful job. So competent. So confident. What a far cry from the sad little wretch I found huddled against the building.*

Cynthia glided to a smooth splashdown and taxied to the dock by the boat ramp. Medics lifted Delbert out onto a stretcher.

"Leave the broken wheelchair on the dock. Close the ramp. I'll turn the plane around to make it easier for Mattie."

She backed the airplane free of the dock, swung it around and came in again. The medics pulled Mattie onto a second stretcher. Told Cynthia they would take them to the Jubilee. She thanked them and taxied out into the lake. In minutes she was airborne again heading north.

Along the way she talked to Air Traffic Control again.

"Can you patch me through to the police or pass a message to them?"

"Give us the message."

"There was a shootout with drug smugglers at Musgrave's Landing on Salt Spring Island. Three of them are dead. They need to send a patrol boat to pick them up."

"Roger, Delboat. We will relay that to the police. Please identify yourself."

"Cynthia Adams, the Pillages' adopted daughter."

"Squawk five five zero zero." She did.

"We have you. Please state your destination and intentions."

"I'm returning to the landing to pick up Officer Lockhart and my mother."

There was quiet for a few minutes.

"Delboat, Victoria Centre. The police have dispatched a patrol boat from Sydney."

"Thank you."

In less than five minutes, the Centre came on again.

"Delboat, Victoria Centre. We are unable to find a record of your pilot's license. Where did you receive it?"

Cynthia ignored the question. She wasn't about to be turned back. A few minutes later she taxied to the dock. Cal grabbed and held the plane, then dropped the ramp.

"A patrol boat has been dispatched to pick these creatures up. Where's Mum?"

"She's inside."

Sylvia emerged from the cottage. When she spotted Cynthia, she ran to her and hugged the girl tightly. She still sobbed.

"What is it, Mum?"

"There's a girl your age in there, dead from an overdose. I keep thinking it could have been you."

"It would be if it weren't for you and Dad."

"Promise me, Thia, you will never touch a drug again."

"You know I won't. You know how important it is for people like you and I, who have lived through tragedy, to enjoy life to the fullest."

"It's so sad…"

"We can't change what happened. We have to live in the present the best we know how and hope that leads to a future we dream about."

Silvia pushed back from the hug and stared at Cynthia. "Where did you acquire such wisdom?"

"From the school of hard knocks. We better go before someone finds out I don't have a pilot's license and leaves the plane stranded here."

Cal stood by watching the exchange, not wanting to interfere. Now he looked startled. "No license?"

"I'm as qualified as any pilot. Dad made sure of that. I just haven't taken the test."

Sylvia regained her composure as they walked to the airplane.

"How are Mattie and Delbert?"

"The medics took them to the Jubilee. Mum, get in. I'll turn the plane around for you, Captain Lockhart. Afraid you will have to sit on the floor on that side."

Cal noticed a patrol boat approaching at full speed.

"I better brief them before we leave."

The boat edged into the end of the dock, careful not to hit a wing. Cal shook hands with the two officers who leaped onto the dock. He explained the situation with the four smugglers and told them about the cash inside. He urged them to look for a drug stash about half a mile up the path. He thought they would find it hidden somewhere close to the path probably sheltered from the weather. They asked if he would stay and help look for it.

"My wife was injured in the shooting. I want to go be with her."

"Okay, we understand. Good work here."

Cynthia turned the plane around while they talked. Cal grabbed onto it, lowered the ramp, climbed in and raised it again. When he sat on the floor, he could barely see out the windshield. The men on the dock shook their heads at the unlikely facsimile of an airplane.

Cynthia backed a little, then swung the nose around to get past the boat. She breathed a sigh of relief when they were underway.

As they passed west of the Pat Bay airport, radio silence was broken again.

"Victoria Centre to Delboat. State your destination."

A meek, "Langford Lake."

"For future reference, an unlicensed pilot is allowed to fly and land an aircraft when the pilot is incapacitated. However, takeoff is not allowed. For the record, this is the only flight you have made today. Tell Delbert to get well soon."

Sylvia reached forward and patted Cynthia on the back.

###

Other Books by Sandy Graham

Life Shattered

Delbert Pillage hides his intelligence through early school years to reduce harassment. Only Sylvia Cairns sides with him and a love is born. His true ability is uncovered in high school and early entry into university separates them. While he is in a summer air force training program, a tragedy pushes her out of his life. He matures into Canada's youngest jet test pilot with all the risk that entails. In this emotion packed story, with his two are shattered … or are they?

Life Threatened

Eight years after "Life Rescued", Cynthia graduates from medical school. Sylvia has become a Public Health Nurse and Delbert provides her with air taxi service into remote coastal villages. Sound placid? It's not. There's a vicious murder to deal with and numerous life-threatening challenges along the way.

The Pizza Dough King

Dino Parelli tells his life story from high school to his dying breath. It's a life marked by successes and tragedies as Dino struggles to win the girl of his dreams, build a business around an unusual niche market, deal with personal losses and cope with old age deterioration. A heart-warming story of enduring love and a lesson in personal and corporate ethics.

Murder – On Salt Spring?

How can there be serious crime on this small island in 1952? Too hard to escape with only a ferry and besides, everyone knows everyone else. In minutes, secrets become common knowledge. Yet, Carl Jenson is found in bed with a knife sticking out of his chest.

Big city detective Mattie Carlyle is sent out to help laid back Cal Lockhart investigate the murder. At loggerheads from the start, can their growing attraction lead to common ground? And can the murder be solved? Can you solve it?

Speak For Me

In a world torn between democracy and dictatorship, can America survive the onslaught of authoritarianism and become once again a beacon of democratic leadership? Emergence of a powerful propaganda machine places the answer in doubt.

A musically gifted extrovert, John McEwan becomes embroiled in this battle, dragging Emma Simon, a deaf introvert, in with him. Forces against them turn violent, driving them into seclusion, tearing them apart, and destroying their rapidly growing company. In a dramatic role reversal, Emma reveals how a strong individual can rise in the face of crises. This emotion-packed novel, at times heart-wrenching, at times heart-filling, lights a path to a brighter future.

A Quiet Rampage

A memoir of my life …so far to age 80.

For more, please visit www.SandysPen.com

Manufactured by Amazon.ca
Bolton, ON